Dr Jacqueline Rule is an Australian author who holds a PhD in English from the University of Sydney, a Bachelor of Arts (Honours) in English from Goldsmiths College, University of London (International Programme) and a Bachelor of Laws from the University of Technology Sydney (UTS). She is the winner of the University of London's 150th Anniversary Prize for academic achievement in English Literature.

Born in South Africa, Jacqueline has lived in Sydney for many years. She is admitted as a solicitor by the Supreme Court of New South Wales.

Jacqueline has worked in research (focusing on law and literature) and academic governance at the University of Technology Sydney (UTS), as an academic tutor teaching literature at the University of Sydney and as a fiction reader for literary journals. Her PhD thesis focused on the intersections between literature and law, narrative ethics and interpretative practices and the representation of historical trauma through the form of the novel.

In addition, Jacqueline spent several years working in a legal organisation, supporting a specialist committee on youth detention in the criminal justice system.

The Leaves is her debut novel.

THE LEAVES

Jacqueline Rule

Aboriginal and Torres Strait Islander readers
are advised that this novel contains representations
of deceased fictional characters

*S*PINIFEX

We respectfully acknowledge the wisdom of Aboriginal and Torres Strait islander peoples and their custodianship of the lands and waterways. The Countries on which Spinifex offices are situated are Djuru, Bunurong and Wurundjeri, Wadawurrung, Gundungarra and Noongar.

First published by Spinifex Press, 2024

Spinifex Press Pty Ltd
PO Box 200, Little River, VIC 3211, Australia
PO Box 105, Mission Beach, QLD 4852, Australia
women@spinifexpress.com.au
www.spinifexpress.com.au

Copyright © Jacqueline Rule, 2024

The moral right of the author has been asserted.

All rights reserved. Without limiting the rights under copyright reserved above, no part of this publication may be reproduced, stored in or introduced into a retrieval system, or transmitted, in any form or by any means (electronic, mechanical, photocopying, recording or otherwise) without prior written permission of both the copyright owner and the above publisher of the book.

Copying for educational purposes: Information in this book may be reproduced in whole or part for study or training purposes, subject to acknowledgement of the source and providing no commercial usage or sale of material occurs. Where copies of part or whole of the book are made under part VB of the *Copyright Act*, the law requires that prescribed procedures be followed. For information contact the Copyright Agency Limited.

No AI Training: Without in any way limiting the author's [and publisher's] exclusive rights under copyright, any use of this publication to 'train' generative artificial intelligence (AI) technologies to generate text is expressly prohibited. The author reserves all rights to license uses of this work for generative AI training and development of machine learning language models.

Edited by Susan Hawthorne and Pauline Hopkins
Cover design by Deb Snibson
Typesetting by Helen Christie, Blue Wren Books
Typeset in Albertina
Printed and bound in Australia by Pegasus Media & Logistics

A catalogue record for this book is available from the National Library of Australia

ISBN: 9781922964021 (paperback)
ISBN: 9781922964038 (ebook)

The paper in this book is FSC® certified. FSC® promotes environmentally responsible, socially beneficial and economically viable management of the world's forests.

before
and

before
and

Past the shadows of cranes and benches and bus stops, past the curve of the footbridge, towards Blackwattle Bay. Over the uneven paving, once a city of pits and chimneys, but now, in early summer, lined with lilac. Terraced streets, their slated roofs and damp jacaranda leaves, curled, clumped, coating the iron-rim of verandahs below.

Near the edge of the park, by the shoreline. Across the dark patches of water—containers, cargo, loaded from warehouses nearby, a power station. In front—small boats in an uneven line, beside a row of jetties. Faith smooths the blanket under a canopy of branches, the leaves of the Port Jackson are small, with a shiny underside of thin felt and rusty brown hairs. Wide spreading, with a large root system, *damun*, rusty fig.

The over-ripe fruit and fallen leaves collect on the ground, sticking to her shoes. Luke's legs are wrestling the air, between his fingers— squashed figs, soil. Faith lies on the grass next to him, pebbles against her back. The fruit is crimson, yellow inside, with hundreds of florets, not as sweet as the sandpaper fig, but she prefers it.

Above them, the unripe fruit are still closed, growing in small pairs, with no stalks. Covering her eyes, giggles, silly faces until long past naptime. Folding the blanket, her bag on her shoulder, strapping him in for the walk home.

A few blocks from their apartment building—yellow concrete, the old incinerator, recently restored. The smokestack now skeletal, empty, sanitised. A 1930s temple, sloped on the shoreline, with rows of vertical columns. For decades, forgotten, but now re-made by the council, stretching to a walkway. A tribute to the end of the rubbish barges, the dumping at sea and backwashing onto beaches. Plaques and signage where thousands of cubic metres, mainly household garbage, evaporated. Not by hand into an open furnace, leaving piles of ash, but lifted, fed into chutes, dissolved. Faith stops, surveilling the Art Deco building. Luke's pram is near the sandstone stairs, the retaining walls.

For weeks after the birth, her body had ached. She feeds him in a wooden rocking chair, by the window of his room. Evelyn had found the chair, dumped in the small lane behind their building. Together they had sanded down the rough splints. Evelyn returned the following day, with a thick grey pillow. The strings curve around the columns at the back to secure the pillow. They're both single mums, though Mitch still sees his dad on weekends. He's two years older than Luke. She's hardly spoken to anyone else in the building. Evelyn hasn't either, and she's been here for almost five years. The pillow takes the edge off the pain, the slow rocking motion helps him sleep.

After his afternoon naps, she takes him down to the grass, in front of their building. She watches him from the bench beneath the jacaranda tree. Evelyn has to work full time, Mitch is in daycare. The jacaranda outside their building is large, with a spreading canopy. Its leaves are delicate, fern-like, with a light green underside that turns brown in the autumn. The trunk is thin, scaly, arched. The twigs have thorns, the flowers grow in thick clusters and for a brief summer bloom, the grass is a gown of violet blue. Soft, feathery. The trumpet-shaped blossoms smother the leaves, soiling the streets. Fallen flowers and seeds litter the path to their front door, blocking the gutters and drains.

The strong root system has spread beyond the path, damaging the fence to the next-door building, displacing other plants, dispersing seeds shipped over from South America many years ago and sold by a visiting sea captain.

In the first trimester, she is nauseous, constantly. Her throat burned from the vomiting, but the pregnancy had set. At four months the queasiness eased, replaced by exhaustion. Towards the end, although it was still spring, she felt unbearably hot, sitting for hours on a chair beside the bath, to ice her feet. Evelyn had helped her down the stairs, carrying towels and a bag for the hospital.

When he's not sleeping, they watch each other. At three months, he begins to smile in his sleep—an involuntary reflex—but she cries nonetheless.

The winter after he turns one, he gets croup. Night after night, she's on the floor beside his cot. Refilling the humidifier, rubbing oil into his chest. Dozing in the rocking chair, under a smear of stars, until his fever subsides with the morning light.

Time bends and crawls. One morning, he surprises her by hoisting himself up against the table and taking his first steps. Weeks later, his unsteady walk becomes a run. Then down the hill at the park, she chases after him. Steering him away from dogs, past joggers and the river, away from the traffic and the older boys skating past, towards the sandpit beside the slide. To a little wooden boat—perched on gravel beside stumps of grass—that they will steer across the harbour. After his bath, with the bedroom lamp on and the balcony door shut tight to keep out the cold air, they look at picture books together.

A yellow tugboat will tow the big ship. Luke drinks warm milk from his sippy cup.

She takes him to the local library. Lifting him on her lap, on a plastic chair, the table streaked with markers. Fingers holding crayons, circular swirls on damp paper. He can draw lions' manes and feathery birds, she's brushing away the sharpenings. Until he catches sight of the small cars and a toy box in the corner and she has to put the book down and follow him.

Around the mat in a plastic fire engine, the wheels catching the carpet. He steps off in frustration; she stands up—her bag tucked against the chair—to soothe his tears. When he tires of puzzles, he sits with her, at the computer.

Tickling his back while she scrolls and clicks, until he falls asleep and, listening to his breathing, her head also nods forward and the words blur on the screen.

On his second birthday, Luke holds Mitch's hand as they chase pirates in the park. The party hats are too tight, they pinch your chin. Evelyn is sitting beside Faith, smoothing the picnic blanket, in the shadow of the tree beside their building. The boys' feet are covered in fallen purple-blue petals. They're collecting on the bench too, squashed and slippery, falling between the slats. She's baked a small cake. They're collecting seedpods from the jacaranda, they're brittle and woody. Mitch rattles a pod, it sounds like a wind chime.

Why don't we put them in my bag?

The sun is reflecting on the branches. Faith is opening her bag to find his play hat. Sap and flowers fall onto the blanket, they're hurrying to close the containers and cover the cake.

The boys have gone to find slugs. There's one wriggling between the slats of the bench. Mitch is holding a small twig. Come, let's light the candles.

They say goodbye on level three.

I'm here, you know, if you need me. Luke pulls Faith's arm towards the steps. There's a smudge of chocolate behind his right ear. Faith is whispering in his ear. Thank you for my present. Evelyn is bending down to hug him, it's a pleasure birthday boy.

Corridors, counters, wall mounted screens, between the entrance and the service desks.

She needs to certify their birth certificates. Months later, they're still processing her application for funds, she's on Parramatta Road, a small box in her handbag. She has to leave the pram at the bottom of the stairs, through the glass: an electric guitar, a drum kit, golf clubs, a stereo, digital clock, a crystal decanter, a tray. He needs a nap, he's grumpy, he's wriggling in her arms. She opens the box, placing the ring and matching earrings on the counter. A brushing of metal against fingertips, an eye pressed against glass.

There's a scratch, back of the earrings have rusted.

I'm not sure they'll sell.

Luke is squeezing her arm, he wants to go down, to look out the window. He's starting to cry.

The face behind the counter pauses, he's watching Luke. The price of silver is down.

She's hurrying back down the stairs, a clean bottle, mixing in the formula, shaking it, strapping him in tucking the envelope into her pocket, reversing the pram back towards the shops, to buy them dinner.

After months of searching between naptime and colouring-in, she finds a job. Mitch's daycare is full, but she finds another one nearby. It's the first day, and she's running late. She's standing at the entrance with his pram, the gate is scraping against the outside mat. She doesn't want him to go inside, to leave her, but he has to. After hugs and a pep talk (for both of them), she walks backwards, smiling as she closes the gate. An elderly carer holding a black cassette player is holding Luke's hand. She'll be back before six.

In another room, she can see rows of low mattresses, empty, with a small pillow and a grey flannel blanket in each, ready for their mid-morning nap.

A see-through fence separates dress-up and hopscotch, afternoon tea and art smocks from the road and an eight-storey building that inks out the sunlight.

There are squeals from the older children, maracas waved in the air. You put your left foot in. You take your left foot out. Standing in the dark pool of the building's shadow, Faith pauses to watch. The older children are allowed the run of the playground, shouting goodbye from the top of the slide or through the window in the chipboard cubby house.

In Luke's room, there are stained cheeks, runny noses. Fifteen minutes later, she is still pressing her face against the gate, squinting to see him through the metal bars.

With their crimson shovels and buckets, pushing little trucks or cars, they follow in a crooked line towards the sandpit. Bouncing up and down to the music, but not Luke. He's stopped crying but he's sitting alone, on top of an old plastic crate, twisting the strings of his play hat. The carers have stepped inside. He squints into the sun, spots her and then howls, until the carer comes back outside and stops the music to come and console him.

Faith runs, past graffiti on the sidewalls of terraces and low-rise buildings, past the old incinerator, its rows of columns reflecting, golden in the sunlight, behind stone stairs and long grass.

She's pausing, to catch her breath, then running towards the bus stop, wiping her nose on her sleeve.

Up the glass-panelled lift to level six. To a plastic partition, fingertips, keyboards, air-conditioning.

Adjusting her swivel chair, her handbag tucked beneath her desk. Behind her, seven years of paperwork, like charcoal headstones, in long rows. She has to clean out the office storeroom, the caretaker will bring a ladder.

Work has cut and diced their hours. Weeks of filing, photocopying and then she's moved, to reception duty on level one.

She longs for the night air when she can push him home from daycare. Facing each other on the uneven pavement, steering the pram around puddles of light. The day lifting off her like a kite as they blow raspberries.

Smiling—as she tucks in his blanket to keep off the wind—beneath a sky of floating yellow balloons.

But the printer cartridge is leaking, the agenda papers are due downstairs in half an hour. There's no answer from the daycare. She arrives, in tears, walking from room to room until she finds him, alone, with the young carer in charge of locking up. The next morning there's an email, from the supervisor. Twice more, and—it won't happen again.

By the time he's four and a half, Luke can hold a pencil, but not well enough to blot the letters of his name.

He chooses his own clothes for preschool, tipping the plastic drawers until he finds his navy t-shirt. He doesn't need help to button-up his flannel pyjamas or put his shoes on for preschool.

At breakfast, he sticks his tongue into the milk of the cereal bowl to make her laugh. But with the other children at preschool, he doesn't speak much. When she fetches him, she has to fill in an incident report. There are bite marks beneath the elbow of his right arm. He has to be able to look after himself.

She takes him for a school readiness assessment, they advise her to keep him back a year.

A few weeks after his sixth birthday, Faith stands at the gates of the local school, enrolments are at capacity, the classroom is a pre-fab demountable.

They stand at the school gates, waiting, beside a cylindrical column, crossed flags, a tilted hat, a soldier in marble and behind, rows and rows of names, all former school mates, brothers, cousins, now attached to plinth and brick.

She's adjusting the straps of his backpack, straightening his play hat. He waves her away, to join the other children in the line.

Mitch shows him around. He can meet him at recess, although he isn't supposed to play with the littlies. His classroom is close to Luke's, at the end of the corridor, by the noticeboard.

Mr Williams doesn't give much homework.

Evelyn takes Mitch earlier, for sport. So, Faith walks him to school, the same time every morning before work.

Carrying his backpack, turning at the old incinerator, then a long straight walk until they get to the school gates. He'd seen something similar, in a book at the library. A yellow castle, he'd thought a church at first, but definitely a castle. With a separate tower behind. He could probably climb it, if he uses the metal frame to lift himself up. He could play hide-and-seek there, with Mitch. They could climb to the top of the tower, a perfect lookout point. But it's closed, his mum says, they aren't allowed to go inside the building. He's going to draw it instead, in waxies or crayons, when they go to the art room after recess. Or he could paint it, in gold or yellow, if he can find his art smock. She's pulling on his arm, gently. They've got to hurry, there's only twenty minutes till the bell rings.

He sits in the same plastic chair every day, it's green with paint stains on the underside. Next to Sammy who pulls his hair and pinches his wax crayons when Mrs Benson (Mrs B) goes out of the classroom for a loo break.

His chair bag is also missing, he crawls under the table to find it. His locker is also next to Sammy's. If you're good, Mrs B will let you ring the bell before school. He's still waiting for his turn.

They have to line up to enter their classroom, balancing their readers and homework diaries, water bottles and morning tea. Mrs B teaches them a rhyming song, about following the rules. She holds up a chart, Sammy knocks his leg under the table.

Try and make silly words with the letters S M C T G P A. Next, words that make sense. Cat. Mop. Cot. None of them make sense. Now things that start with the first letter of your name.

Mrs B divides them into pairs.

They have to sit quietly together and look for dots and spaces. Samuel is pulling silly faces. Before lunchtime, Mrs B reads them a story about a crocodile.

All the animals are too afraid to clean their teeth.

The children have to guess what will happen next. Luke zips up his pencil case. He doesn't like crocodiles.

Read the pictures. Read the words. Tell the story.

Luke leans backwards, the front legs of his chair are off the floor.

In pairs now. Elbow to elbow, knee to knee, book in the middle so we both can see.

Mrs B turns back to the whiteboard. Samuel elbows him in the stomach. Trace and copy. Nine is like a backwards P. His fingers hurt. Loops and dots and downward movements. She stands beside him. Keep your feet on the floor, hold the pencil firmly. Follow the direction of the arrows. Sloping lines to make a capital 'V'. He wants to colour in the picture of a vase but Mrs B says wait till the end.

The terms are flying, he's forgotten his clothes for PE again.

When the afternoon bell rings, Mrs B walks the remaining children across the outside corridor to a different classroom for kids' club. He sits by himself near the window. The clip inside his homework diary pinches his thumb when he turns the pages.

An older girl at the table next to him is decorating a paper mask. Feathers and beads and patches of glue under her elbow, then on the side of the table. On rainy afternoons they watch movies. When Faith arrives, Sammy and him are the only ones left.

On the way home, they stop at the park, near the water. The figs have ripened. They sit, shaded under the branches, between the fallen fruit. He takes his homework folder out of his bag, to show her his new reader.

She's impressed with his reading, he's made so much progress. He's leaning against her.

She picks up a small pair of figs, he wants to try too. It's not very sweet, but he likes it. Crimson, on the inside—yellow, with tiny florets. After he's chewed it, he leaves the slightly bitter skin and the stalk on the ground, for the birds.

Mrs B says they should start packing and unpacking their school bags themselves and preparing their uniforms. At home, Faith opens the lid of the kitchen bin for crusts and apple cores, she shows him how to wipe the inside of his lunchbox. With shoes, two yellow cloths and polish, they sit together on the carpet, one shoe each.

He's big now, he doesn't have to be afraid of the dark. But he still wakes up in the night. She's lying on the floor, next to his bed. The room is silent, but he can hear noises. From the roof, his cupboard. Her back is stiff.

Once he's asleep, she's up, closing the door behind her, trying not to click the door handle.

Every morning, pausing at the yellow castle—adjusting the straps—walking arm in arm, his school bag shifting up and down, until they say goodbye as at the school gate. She's hugging him, he pulls away slightly as a group of year ones pass. He shouldn't care what they think. She's going to give him a goodbye kiss, and no chit-chat in class today. Show Mrs B how well you can do your readers. He's walking the stone path, away from the gate, and the sports field, towards his classroom. What if someone lives in the yellow tower, secretly, someone bad or on the run? He needs to bring Mitch with him, to make sure.

Line up, follow the stairs to your locker.

It's Sammy's birthday, he's got lollies for the whole class in his bag. His cousins are coming over for dinner and cake. Quieten down please and take out your pencil cases. Put up your hand if you've forgotten your ruler. Thin, thinner, thick, thicker, tall, long, short, deep, shallow, long, longer, longest. He'll give everyone a lolly, but he won't give Luke one. He's sticking out his tongue. Luke kicks his chair, from behind. Mrs B stops the class and writes Luke's name on the board. A girl behind him is chatting, another boy drops his pencil case and nearly falls out of his seat picking it up. Please everyone, Sammy won't hand out any lollies if this continues. And stop leaning back on your chairs.

After the term break, his classroom looks different.

Mrs B has taken down their artworks, the shelves are tidy. They're going to start a new project this term. They can take their old pictures home now.

Please collect them from the red box before the bell rings and try not to scrunch them in your bags.

Faith's manager is waiting at her desk when she arrives. They're sitting in his office, he's swivelling his chair. They have her details on file, they would have liked to keep her on. But there's just no budget, they're all in the same boat. His phone is ringing, he's apologising, she's showing herself out of the office. Someone has organised a farewell card, there's an empty cardboard box beside her chair. She arrives early to fetch Luke, before the bell rings. She's waiting to the side of the fence, trying not to cry. A toddler is running towards the plants, to be picked up again moments later. The bell is like a siren. Older siblings arrive, there are flung school bags, lost play hats beside the fence, crumpled paper, lunchboxes. Luke's class is still lining up at the end of the corridor, when she catches his eye. He shouts and runs towards her, gesturing to the picture in his hand.

His fingers are covered in dried paint.

Surely she can guess? It's the yellow castle, there's the tower, the colours smudged a bit (because Sammy knocked his arm). She can make out the columns and the stairs. He's added a moat and a drawbridge,

Mrs B said it's very creative. I told her we live near the castle. It's a beautiful painting, he's very talented. She can hold it for him, till they get home, so it doesn't bend. They could put it up the wall, with some tape or Blu-Tack. If he can wait a few days till she goes to the shops.

He's smiling, nodding, skipping ahead of her.

More interviews, leather armchairs, or plastic chairs, behind a machine that dispenses instant coffee, or hot chocolate. Afterwards, Faith heads back to the library, to the extra computer and the elderly librarian, who asks after Luke. He's a schoolboy now. Black dots and spots and lines. Listening to gurgles and intermittent cries from the children's section, beside the computers, as mothers rock their prams, one-handed, reading. She cancels after-school care to save money. He doesn't even like it, he'd rather be with her. On those afternoons, hand in hand—jumping between shadows on the pavement—they run. The straps of his school bag against her left shoulder. Past the fence at the edge of the sports field, past the fire station and the across the footbridge. Cartwheels, gravelly palms, a stray ball. He's too big for the slide, he can hang upside down on the monkey bars. He's barefoot at the top of the climbing net, or rolling down the sloping grass. Soil is stuck to his knees, he's still got a sandwich left in his lunchbox. They never give them enough time to eat. She's asking about his day. He's twisting the chain on the swing to make it spin, it leaves rust marks on his fingertips. Sammy got in trouble again, he had to write me a sorry note.

Two months later, when she fetches him, it's too cold for the park.

She has sold her last necklace, a watch, some small furniture. At night, she walks between the narrow rooms turning off all the lights, except the small lamp beside her files. She's leaning over the stovetop in her dressing gown, her heels against the granite tiles. The rent is the most important, she has to pay that first. She bleaches his school shirt in the green bucket in the corner of the shower. She is distraught when he misplaces his PE clothes, he will have to play in his uniform.

Sammy is home with chickenpox.

Some days she is too tired to go to the library. She snaps at him when he pours too much milk. It's a waste, I'll finish your bowl. At night, she lies awake—listening for him—making a mental list of their possessions. She has nothing left that would sell. Sammy is still spotty, but he's back at school.

At the end of recess, Mrs B calls Luke aside. What happened?

He sits opposite her at the front of the classroom, she hands him a tissue. The whiteboard is full of writing, Sammy started it. He was defending himself. She understands, it was Mr James' decision, not hers.

He's blowing his nose, he can tell she's disappointed.

It's not fair, he made me sit in the reflection chair, it should have been Sammy.

Two wrongs don't make a right, but she'll talk to Mr James.

He couldn't concentrate at the back of the classroom, Sammy kept turning around and sticking out his tongue, Mr James didn't stop him doing that!

They're all still looking at him, whispering, when they walk out in lines. He has blood on his collar, a bruised lip.

Mum is waiting at the gate. He's still crying, his eyes are stinging. They're going to have a talk, but not here, she lifts his backpack off the ground, carrying it on her shoulder, towards the castle, home.

She's in the bathroom, Luke slams his door. He sits on the edge of the bed, reaching for a small metal car, throwing it, off the shelf, against the wall, a plastic wheel, off. He sits on the floor, beside his bed, holding the wheel. She comes in, she's not angry, a bit disappointed, but he's had a tough day at school, she can glue it on again. She sits on the floor, next to him, he climbs onto her lap, leaning his head against her. Sammy told him he was ugly, because of his skin, because it's mixed. They sit on the carpet, hugging, that's a lie, he's the opposite of ugly, the opposite, she's reaching for his arm, she's going to talk to Mrs B about Sammy, and the principal too, he's in bed now, she's fixing the blanket, he doesn't mention the broken car again, his breathing is getting heavier, he's almost asleep, she's still on the floor beside him, gently reaching for the lamp.

She falls asleep too, most nights, on the floor beside Luke's bed or at the table where they eat, her head and neck, drooping down, forwards, towards the piles of letters, resumes, unpaid bills, papers, like a patchwork quilt, to be moved again, before breakfast.

He's up early, the next morning, pulling at her sleeve.

He's feeling much better but she can't move, her neck, her head is sore, burning. He needs the toilet, there's a funny sound in his room. He's opening her eyelids with his fingers. I want to read a story, before breakfast. She's turning on the light in the bathroom, sorry my boy—Mum's not feeling well today—his pyjama top is over his head—it makes his skin itch, he doesn't want to put on his uniform yet, he'll spill. His dressing gown is on a hook on the back of the bathroom door, but he can't reach it. You should go to the doctor, Mum.

She walks so slowly that he's going to be late for assembly. She's pausing by the old incinerator to catch her breath, holding onto the railing, at the bottom of the sandstone stairs, looking up at the columns, the edges, the tower.

She sits on the ground at the school gate. There's no one else around. Her cheeks are flushed, he's running towards the office to fetch a late slip. The straps on his bag have twisted again, he'll ask Mrs B to help him.

She walks back from school too, to save the bus fare, but not today. She sits on an empty corner of the bus stop bench. Waiting until a teenage girl with a cap stands up as the bus approaches. It's not a long ride. Ten minutes, in traffic. She can make it, if she doesn't close her eyes.

She's sweating when she gets to the top of the stairs.

She finds the thermometer, in the bathroom cupboard, it's under her tongue now. With a damp towel around her waist, closing her eyes—

When she finally wakes up, it is after 2 p.m. He's the only child left at the school gate. Mrs B is standing beside him.

He's cross with her, for being late, but not for long.

At home, he changes out of his uniform, leaving his clothes on the floor beside the couch, she owes him a TV show. She nods, reaching for his bathroom stool, a wet facecloth. A bottle of cold water, on the floor beside her bed. Just a few episodes, while she has a nap.

He's bored, after the third episode. She's still asleep. He feels bad, maybe she is very sick. He sits at his green wooden table in his room. Scrap paper, scissors, glue.

GET WELL SOONE MUM!

He places the card on the floor beside her clothes. Then he's climbing into bed next to her—in his pyjamas, with his pillow.

The next morning, Luke carries his wooden chair to the front door, leaning it against the door to keep it open. Then down the stairs, to find Evelyn, but there's no answer. He writes a note, tucking it under their door.

He knows how to make cereal and he can peel bananas. He eats two on the couch, under a blanket. Mrs B will be wondering where he is. He's watching the lull of her head, the sweat above her lip. He's holding the cup towards her, the water spilling on her sheet.

They've run out of milk. He turns the carton over, shaking it until the drops fall on the edge of his tongue.

He tiptoes in and out of her room. She's rolled over on her other side, he feels her forehead. Even the TV doesn't wake her. In the morning, she finally sits up—her back still baking—against the pillows and calls to him. The cord of the blinds are protruding, unclipped, knotted between the fingers of the white cable running from the wall to her bedside lamp. Her knees are folded into the pale skin of the mattress. She's gesturing to him, he's reaching for the wooden frame. Pulling himself up until he's beside her, the cord of the blind in his hands. He's opening the blinds slowly, dissolving them into day. A few blocks away, he can just make out the yellow columns of the castle, the smooth round neck of the tower.

A little later, knocking. She just saw his note on the front door. Cereal mostly. No, he hasn't been at school, his mum is very sick, more than before. Evelyn is unfolding a tissue from her handbag. Following him down the corridor, towards her room. Reaching for her phone.

He's pressing his face against her arm, watching as they carry her down the stairs. To the ambulance. Night, two levels below. Mitch has more toys.

Above them, a pale sheet, suspended from the corner of the headboard across the bedroom, tied to the bars of the window. Inside the makeshift tent—two boys, cross-legged, waiting. Mitch's pyjamas are too long for him. The cuffs fall over Luke's hands. He flaps them out of the way to turn his cards over. Mitch's pile is bigger.

Dinner is ready boys. Just roll them up Luke. Come on, before it gets cold.

He's lying on a mattress beside Mitch's bed. Tracing the outline of his cupboard, tiptoeing towards the gap in the blinds. His nose against the glass. The street outside is faint, smudged. He turns the pillow over, maybe he'll sleep better on the other side. Evelyn will take him to the hospital after school.

At recess the next morning, Mrs B wants him to eat his sandwich inside so they can chat. He gets to cuddle Little Cat. She sits on top of a special bookshelf and loves to learn.

Mrs B missed him, she was worried.

The principal has come too, into Mrs B's classroom, to speak to him. They want to hear what happened to his mum. Sitting across the desk from him, Mrs B's nose is scrunching up into a little ball while she listens. The principal is leaning against the chalkboard, taking notes.

The next morning, Mrs B is waiting to speak to Evelyn at the school gate. They are still chatting when he waves goodbye to Mitch beside the demountable classrooms.

Outside the hospital: taxis, a park, flashing lights, figures carved in cement. A revolving door. Evelyn gently tugging his arm, steering them towards the front desk. Clipboards, coats, a milk-white corridor, peering through half-opened door frames. A basin, a sign in red font, lucky pebble between his palms, pushing against a grey handle.

Six beds, a high ceiling. Behind the door—a cross, white folds of material to partition the patients—Evelyn sits. Halfway between the foot of the bed and the curtain. Reaching for Luke's arm as he throws himself onto Faith's bed. Pulling him back, so that the nurse can take her blood pressure.

Mrs B says when people are ill you have to say an extra little prayer before you fall asleep. Besides, her eyes are closed, fast asleep, so she can't be saying any prayers herself. Evelyn and the doctor are talking.

Behind the curtain, scratchy material against his back. He should build a tent, surprise her when she comes home. Sitting underneath in the dark with a torch and his favourite story. Maybe she'll let him stay up late on a school night.

All week, instead of lining up to bounce tennis balls against the back of the gymnasium, he joins the girls for Lunch and Library. In the library, you can do anything except eat (you do that beforehand). You have to pack away the arts and crafts box five minutes before the bell rings. Tracy is in his group sometimes. She likes the special card he has made for Mum.

But it looks a bit girlish now with the hearts she added.

She was only trying to help. He turns away to talk to his other friends. You should have asked first, she's not your mum.

Mitch spends half of every week at his dad's apartment. Evelyn insists that he use his knife and fork properly and only lets Mitch have sweets on a Sunday, when he gets home from his dad's.

She's always at the school gate early. The three of them walk home together, the same route he walked with Mum before she got ill. He asks Evelyn if he can stop at the castle, to look at the tower. She doesn't understand, he'll show her, he knows the way. It's near the water.

Oh yes, she says nodding, I know the yellow castle.

Mitch is bored, he's sitting on the sandstone steps beside the old incinerator, dribbling a ball. He shows Evelyn the tower, where someone, dangerous perhaps, might be hiding. It could be hundreds of years old, a mediaeval fortress, still standing by the foreshore. She surveys the building, she doesn't want to hurt his feelings. Mitch is rolling his eyes. She's standing near the plaques, Luke is still learning to read. Rag-pickers, the quarries and soot, the tin smelters that came before. The wrappers, leftover bones, nightsoil and broken bottles littering the streets. Despite their toxic fumes, they were better, surely, than all that? Efficient, modern, clean. With a reverberatory furnace, a grabber, a moveable crane, rubbish tipped the chutes, heated in the air and dissipated.

Solid, liquid, light, heat.

Mitch lets him have the ball, just for the way home, he already knows how to dribble it, he's been watching. Evelyn is impressed, he could join the school team too, Mitch is walking ahead of them, he doesn't turn around. She likes them to eat dinner at the table, but they can watch TV on the couch tonight. Evelyn is balancing her plate, she folds her legs and adjusts the straps of her dressing gown between mouthfuls. She works most days and some weekends. Mitch's dad works on a building site twenty minutes from the city. Mitch has never been up one of those cranes, but he's going to take him. Most of his day is just standing around, waiting for permission to start up the crane.

If Luke does his readers after dinner, they can watch a bit more TV. Mitch's dad gave him a yellow vest, like the one he wears at work. It's bright and reaches down to his knees.

The hospital garden behind her ward is a small courtyard with a row of pot plants and some stone benches beneath a 'No Smoking' sign.

Faith is so weak that Evelyn borrows a hospital wheelchair. With Luke beside them she pushes Faith, between the linen baskets and cleaning trolleys, towards the double glass doors leading outside. One afternoon, when he is in the garden alone, Luke looks around and breaks the stems off the plants, the tips feel rubbery under his palms.

The stalks don't fit in the pocket of his school shorts. He hides them, behind the garbage bins.

On colder afternoons, once she is strong enough, they stand on either side of her chair and lift her under her elbows. She walks slowly, behind them, in the fluorescent corridor.

Sister's orders.

Back and forth, until she is breathless and pleads to return to her room.

A few days later, Evelyn is in the kitchen. There's mince and sautéed onion, a wooden spoon. In the bedroom, beneath their tent, Mitch is holding a small box of semi-precious stones, he took them to show Luke. His half-sister won't miss them for a couple of days.

There's a knock.

The wooden spoon is on the board, she turns off the gas.

No, I'm not his mother. We were about to have dinner.

Luke, could you come here for a minute please. There's somebody who wants to talk to you.

Her hair is reddish brown, she has speckled glasses like a tiger's eye. She speaks like Mrs B but doesn't smile. She asks a lot of questions. He tells her about the tent they made in Luke's room (not about the precious stones that Mitch took though) and how his mum is ill and that the hospital has a garden (a small one). But it does have a few flowers.

Mrs B has a special class toy, a cat, that only he got to play with.

Evelyn's couch is comfier than the one at home.

The brown fabric has lots of scratches but it's soft enough to sleep on. There's a small space where you can wiggle your toes into the material under the armrest. She is watching him, waiting for an answer, but he didn't hear the question. She repeats herself. Oh, yes, Mum is very kind, she's the best. He knows, she's very ill, but she's going to get better soon. No, he can't remember what he ate, different things, from the cupboard. He even made Mum food.

She fetches the keys, Luke follows, the social worker walks slowly behind them.

Evelyn had only been into the apartment once, since Faith went to hospital, to fetch a few things for Luke, wash up and take out the rubbish. A black bag with plastic yellow bow that had stunk of vomit and stale milk. She'd washed a pile of dirty plates before the cockroaches got to them. It seemed empty now, not clean, but not how it had been either. She's pulling on the blind cords, turning on the lights to survey each room for her notebook. Faith's bed is unmade, there are piles of washing and a scratchy grey blanket and pillow, on the floor beside the bed. Where he must have slept. She opens drawers, cupboards, bathroom cabinets, scribbling new notes in every room.

Then silent, single file, back down the stairs back to Evelyn's.

You go on inside Luke, tell Mitch I'll be in soon. Luke runs into the bedroom, beneath the sheeted canopy, biting the skin around his nails.

You can hold the treasure box if you want to.

He's curling himself into a ball.

What did she want?

He's crying softly beneath the blanket, but loud enough for Mitch to hear.

Hey, do you want a rematch? Re-match? You're getting better.

I want Mum.

Come on Luke, your mum's in the hospital, that's why you're with us.

Mum.

Evelyn is back inside, she's lifting the flap to the make-shift tent, she can't fit inside.

It's ok, she's gone, she's gone now.

He can't sleep.

Ouch, that was my leg.

Sorry, I needed the toilet.

Outside—hard hats, bending shadows. Glowing vests, luminous orange against the grey. An open manhole, exposed wires, a temporary enclosure. An arm waving from a neighbour's balcony, towards the workmen.

Drowned words. Swallowed by the shriek of drills.

Tiger's Eye, her glasses, her hair. She's in his classroom, standing at the back. Watching him, silently, while Mrs B writes maths sums on the board.

Morning. Evelyn is shuffling past his mattress to draw back the curtains.

We'll go after school today Luke, I promise. Please can you boys get up.

A foot edges out.

Just five more minutes. Mitch can go ahead.

Come on buddy.

He can hear her, but his head is still under the blanket.

Please, otherwise we'll be late.

He can take his ball with him, for the hospital garden, not inside her room, not along the corridors. A girl with her leg in plaster presses the button first, a red glow, doors closing, more pings, squeezing his hand and then they are out, on level three.

Mum's room first, ok. And keep away from the glass.

They are empty today—the other five beds—

No need to close the partition or tiptoe from the door towards her bed beside the dark blue window frame. She doesn't lift her head today when he calls out. Or sit up and hug him or ask if Sammy is giving trouble and if he has done his homework and washed his hands properly. Or press the small button next to her drip to ask the nurse to prop up her pillows or bring her a glass of orange juice. Or say anything that either of them can understand, she only mutters and sways her head against her pillow until it is Evelyn who presses a finger against the bell.

Go and play outside Luke, please. Go. And watch the windows. Ok? I'll come get you when Mum is more awake.

A doctor's coat, walls, tiles, ceiling.

Faith. Can you lift your head for me please. Just a little bit. Try talking up a little. The nurse is going to help you sit up now. We'll just change the bed linen and then you can rest. I met your son today; he's a good boy. I'll be back to check on you later.

Luke is walking back to the garden. Moving aside for a trolley piled with linen, following white coats down the corridor. He's outside, watching them talk, behind the glass doors.

Please, just tell me.

The doctor is rubbing his hands together until the foam dissolves. Returning the clipboard with its string in place. His hands folded into his overcoat. I'm sorry Evelyn. The meningitis has caused a systemic infection. We are doing all we can to keep her hydrated and comfortable.

The nurse beside him is still holding the tray of food, untouched. Shaking her head, It's in God's hands now.

His tummy is sore, the garden stinks of smoke, he wants to go home.

Three slips into four, five. They're still at the hospital, Luke is hungry, his left hand is sore, he knocked it with the ball.

Have it, please. The nurse will bring her dinner soon anyway.

The tomatoes are pale, damp. He pulls out two slices of cheese. At least they give sick people jelly.

Mitch is on the couch watching cartoons with his dad when they get back. Evelyn heads straight to the kitchen to warm up the take-aways.

He's already eaten.

Ok, thanks.

See you, my boy.

Mitch is hugging his father, the front door is closing. The boys head back to their room. Mitch is a bit down, after the visit. They're sitting together on the floor, playing cars. He's really lucky. Even if he only sees him every few weeks. Luke has never met his dad. Half an hour later: they're asleep, on the TV: a documentary, ads, the late night news. Beside the couch—Evelyn on her knees, weeping.

Visiting hours at the hospital are over, the passage lights only turn on with sensors. You'd have to squint to see the faces of the sisters, hanging inside their rectangular frame beside her hospital room. Five apparitions, veiled in white. In the front row, at chest-height, their rosary beads partially obscured. Behind them, six nuns with black veils.

The figure in the centre towers above them. Most of them wear glasses. Only one, at the bottom left of the frame (with a prominent mole beside her nose) is smiling. It was taken in Dublin. Years before the sisters were shipped off to the colony, at the request of the Bishop.

Coffee is in the kitchen beside the corridor. A fluorescent glow from bathroom doors, half open as night-staff conduct their midnight rounds. The faint snore of traffic through closed windows. The nurse is checking Faith's pulse, her blood pressure, then closing the door for the night.

The fluorescent light in Faith's hospital room is slightly dimmed, there's intermittent blinking at the base of the drip.

Faith is six months pregnant, lying on the couch in Evelyn's apartment. She's breathing heavily, her eyes are stinging. Evelyn is passing Faith a box of tissues, sitting on the couch beside her friend.

Like Evelyn, Faith was also a blanket baby—part of the Stolen Generations, they told her—eventually. One of the later ones, but not the last. The nurse would have hidden her, under a hospital blanket, though it was the middle of summer. Telling her Aboriginal mother that she was stillborn, or that she died immediately after the birth. Or perhaps they drugged her, or tied her to the bed in the maternity ward and didn't tell her anything.

She grew up in foster homes. When she was old enough to ask, they said her mother died in childbirth.

She still doesn't know her mother's real name, or her father's, or if she has brothers, sisters, cousins.

At eighteen, she called the hospital, they referred her to a case worker, a new network that had been formed.

But without a surname, not even her mother's first name, Faith's past was stolen. Her file could not be located.

Evelyn is passing her a damp cloth, holding her hand; Faith is shaking, she doesn't want to upset the baby who she can feel kicking inside her.

Evelyn is holding Faith's hand, but she's also crying, for her own mother. Evelyn's mother—who was told she had no other family, that she was 'lucky' to have a chance to make something of her life. Who was taught only English, how to be a good Christian, who was beaten till she bled if she asked questions. After the children's home, she was sent to a training college. Given a thin file, with a few photographs stuck to the pages, and birthday cards, letters that she had never seen. There was no reunion, Evelyn's grandmother had already passed, she only managed to track down some distant cousins.

Evelyn's mother, who still found the strength to care for, and raise and love her own child, with every fibre of her being, and to pass that deep, inextinguishable love on to Evelyn.

They're still sitting on the couch, it's mid-afternoon. She's hugging Faith, she's knows she's going to be a wonderful mother.

Faith falls asleep, her knees curled towards her bump. Evelyn covers her with a blanket. When she wakes up, it's evening.

Her eyes are puffy, she can barely open them. Evelyn stays to make her dinner, Mitch is already asleep in his cot.

Light. Alarms. Curtains.

Luke, your mum needs to rest today. Muffled sounds, from his mattress.

His cheeks are wet. I know, I know.

Evelyn is sitting on the edge of the mattress. Mitch is rolling his eyes, but still joining in the hug. I understand Luke, it's not easy. Now come on, you too are going to need a late slip if we don't hurry.

Flakes dissolving into milk.

It's all right, you don't have to eat if you feel ill.

The nurse is standing beside Faith. Her eyes are closed, she's saying something, but she can't make it out, the line on the screen is up, down, down, she's not responding, her pulse is weakening, the nurse is pressing the alarm, calling for the doctor, her colleague enters, he's in the other ward, on his rounds, just call him, urgently, come now.

Faith's been in labour for hours, the lower half of her body is numbed, dulling the intense contractions.

They're pumping oxytocin to speed it up, they're worried about his breathing, another midwife and doctor has joined them. She's trying to push but she can feel nothing. She's watching the line on the screen, he's going to be ok, he's going to, they're reaching for him, with forceps, then suddenly, a cry—he's with her—her boy, her boy. Her own breath is stabilising, it's just before dawn. He's tiny, perfect, just a few seconds old, weighed, wrapped, healthy, lying on her chest in the hospital bed. The nurse is opening the curtains, they're watching the sun rise, together, warm, skin to skin. She will call him—Luke, her boy—

She strokes the creases in his forehead, his little head still is cone-shaped, dried blood coats the wound where they cut the cord. Beside her bed, a bassinet, a navy blanket, a label affixed to the side. She had walked in a daze to the bathroom, nearly fainting in the shower, from the blood loss, the exhaustion, her legs are shaky. Her elbow is gripping the door handle, she's stumbling towards the crib—beside her bed—towards him, she's happy, calm despite the pain and the stitches and the fluorescent lights.

When she pulls back the curtains, it is still morning, the street is violet, lavender, blue. A thick coat of jacaranda petals, enfolding the pavement.

It's their first night together, watching each other. Hourly cries in the darkness—the pain as she leans sideways, cradles him, in her hospital bed, singing to him—sometimes with her eyes closed. Tracing the outline of his toes, his hands, the shape of his ears, the hospital tag around his right ankle. Placing him gently in the bassinet, while she limps to the bathroom.

The nurse is demonstrating, how to hold him, swaddle him. He's a good weight. There's a plastic nappy bag— twice-knotted— in the bin beside the door. The woman she shares a room with is excited about the night nursery, the nurse wheels the bassinet in for feeding, and out again, in two-hour increments. But she won't let them take Luke there. Besides, she won't sleep anyway—she's smiling at the elderly nurse—she doesn't need more painkillers.

There's a hearing test for him. Classes, feeding and sleep schedules—she'll go once the pain has eased a bit—and the daily check-ups for

Luke, for her. She's in a line behind three other mothers, they're in their nighties, some with dressing gowns, pushing their bassinets along the passages. She's waiting for the nurse to help them with the first bath. He squeals, momentarily. Then it's over, he's wrapped and wheeled back to the hospital room, for another feed.

Handover—morning staff—orange juice, cereal, a carton of UHT milk, a croissant not entirely thawed, nurses on their first rounds, entering, leaving. In the room: white coats, machines, raised voices, a heart rate monitor, still affixed to her fingertips, then removed—

—skipping ropes, a plastic crate,   beside the playground,
                                                                at Luke's school,
rackets, balls, hula hoops, two nets full
The Principal and Mrs B, walking in unison,
                         Evelyn a few steps behind, Luke, alone,

behind   the cubby house, on the   concrete,
               under the gazebo.   Little Cat clutched, under the
teacher's arm.
Evelyn on one side,   Mrs B on the other
the Principal
   a few metres back
curious faces,   pressed,
        to the window,
a hand,   on Luke's shoulder
the toy, against   his chin,
across the road,   the jacaranda trees are bare,

their ferny leaves   yellow,   loosened,
                             discarded.

The hospital office.

A chipboard desk, Evelyn squinting through the window, towards the city, the buildings like raised arms, lined up, stretching.

A habit, from hairline to floor.

Reflected in the closed doors of a filing cabinet, mahogany wood, glasses.

Ink globules smudging on white.

The nun's hand, resting on the page.

Six or seven thousand dollars, minimum, for the funeral.

Facing down, picking at the flap of skin beside her thumb nail.

I'm sorry, I can't afford it.

Anyone else? Siblings, parents? Other friends? Evelyn is shaking her head, her eyes scanning the files, medical dictionaries, events, fundraising, thirty years of service archived behind glass, the rosary around her neck, behind the door. On the wall, in the front row, framed, beside the Mother Superior. Thirty nursing graduates, cross-legged, smiling, with identical black shoes, the stained glass of the chapel behind.

There is an alternative, Evelyn.

I'm sorry Sister. I couldn't do it to her, she wanted to be buried.

The nun is excusing herself, for a word with her supervisor.

Her white folds brushing the carpet as she walks. Evelyn sits alone, with the picture of the smiling young nurses.

Fifteen minutes later she's back. Evelyn pulls her chair closer to the desk.

I've spoken with the Local Health District. We can assist you to make arrangements. It will be basic though. We can provide the casket and the hearse. A minister will attend to oversee the burial. And if there's anyone else, could you please ...

She's nodding, biting her thumb. Please thank them and the doctor.

One more thing, Evelyn.

Unfortunately, they can't provide a headstone, and she is going be placed ... with others. But there will be a number, for the grave I mean, and it will be a dignified resting place.

Her chair, stuttering as she rises, she's pulling on the string of her handbag.

It will be somewhere. You will be able visit her.

A door handle, the mid-morning light, sliced, quartered, reflected.

The following Monday—Evelyn, two boys, one hand each, at the back of the queue for the ticket booth, Central Station. A hand stretched across the booth. Platform 18, you'll need to change trains. It's a ten-minute walk. She's emptying some small change into Evelyn's palm.

Fluorescent lights, a newsagency at the entrance to a long tunnel for commuters, buried beneath the station. The historic tiles are stained with food scraps and dried urine, commuters keep to the middle, beneath the flickering tubes. On both edges of the tunnel, crates, backpacks, sleeping bags, cardboard signs, a shopping trolley piled high with canvas bags. A young woman, mid-twenties, pregnant, is on her knees, beside a sleeping bag and an empty hat. She can't go back home, anything will help; the hostel costs thirty dollars a night. Beside the railing of the stairs, another woman in a faded grey and black tracksuit leans against the wall, she looks like a grandmother, but she has no shoes, just a pair of bright yellow socks and a small backpack on her lap. Two police officers are standing over, leaning towards her, gesturing.

Come on boys.

They follow Evelyn a few paces towards the steps down to the platform.

Wait, can we? She nods, Luke turns around, with the coins in his hand, but the homeless woman with the yellow socks is gone.

The train is full, students mostly, headed to their satellite campus.

Hands please, hold the rail.

It smells funny in here.
Behind the yellow line, boys.
CentralRedfernBurwoodStrathfieldLidcombe.
Eight minutes.
Seven minutes. Mum, I'm hungry.
A low strider, then a shrill cry. Headlights, rattling cables overhead.
Beneath them, fraying red folds of material. Luke's head against her shoulder. Mitch to her left.
On her lap, empty black squares, size eleven font. When the boys have gone to bed. When she can face it. Within seven days, counting today.

- Female
- Sydney, New South Wales
- Office Administration
- Single
- A son
- Rookwood

Beneath the forms, a map and historical brochure. January 1865: the first run on the Cemetery Line to Haslem's Creek, the necropolis. Then twice a day, a special platform area for mourners, coffins. Vanished, except for some short sections of track.

Would you like a sip of water?
   He doesn't, Mum.
   Let him answer for himself.
   Luke?
   Knees to chest. Spine flat, head upright now, arms scratchy against the slits and bursting sponge.
   She loved you, so much. More than anything.
   He's tracing word patterns into the skin of the chair.
   We have to say a proper goodbye today. All of us.
   Strands of hair are stuck to the edges of her scarf.
   ~~CentralRedfernBurwoodStrathfield~~Lidcombe.

Quickly, watch the stairs. Mitch, say excuse me please. Careful of the gap.

I want chips, from the vending machine.

Mesh fence, gravel.

Raised walkway, signage, bars. Navy blue on white. Yellow barriers, stairs. Descending arms, slanting on a silver cross, hand rails.

Please don't run.

Luke, take Mitch's hand.

Post office, newsagent, lounge—open 24/7. Brick houses, one with a white balcony, green shutters. Glass. Flags, above the roof of the Railway Hotel.

Railway Street cross east, to the Lidcombe entrance, past Mortuary Station—long out of use.

chapels cottages offices lawns crypts eternal rest rose garden None Many mausoleums flowers war graves memorial walk

Crooked, slanting. Baked marble. Stone.

Seated, under a tree.

Come, I'll carry you. Please Luke. The Minister will be there already.

Along a path, then grass, stone.

Piercing the soil: sunburnt crosses, sticks, remnants of petals, ribbon, stems.

Beside a shrub, white flaps billowing.

Sister, you came.

Bending down, there's a hand on his shoulder.

God is looking after her.

Evelyn is helping him wipe his nose. The tips of the Minister's robes are damp, muddy.

The coffin is wooden, with plastic handles. A flat lid.

Let us pray.

An outline, white calico shroud.

May the Church be a comforting witness to Christ, to us all.

Hands, squeezing her wrists.

For the grieving, for the sick, the dying, for those who rest with the Lord.

Plywood into soiled earth.

For a mother, for a son. For those who cared for her in her illness. Comfort one another in this time of grief.

May she be judged in mercy.

Pebbled, a garland of weeds and long grass.

Nauseous, smudged, streaming. Towards the gates, the station. Luke's feet around her waist, head over her shoulder, eyes closed. Mitch's arm around the narrow strap of her bag.

How come I have to walk?

Don't wake him Mitch. Besides, you're too big.

So is he.

A tissue, unfolded. Rough against the sides of her nostrils.

Do you think they can hear us Mum?

Who?

Half an hour later, black clothes on a bench. The bus stop, across from the station. On their laps—lunch, three boxes, rectangular, with a raised oval flap—paper teeth piercing the folds.

Try not to use your hands boys.

I don't want any more.

You sure Luke?

My tummy's sore.

Let's head home boys. You can rest on the train.

Hands against paper, enclosing the plastic fork, closing the flap, fixing the teeth into position, shaking crumbs from his trousers, standing.

White lines, watching as cars slow. Then up, to the platform, arms outstretched, behind her, one hand each.

Across the road—rubbish stuck to the pavement; a takeaway box, not empty, but damp, suspended against the mouth of the bin.

One week. Two days off school, three days back.
    Luke's bag over Evelyn's shoulder, Mitch on the sports field.
    Just give me five minutes with Mrs B please.
    Nodding, running, then emerging to watch them through the cubby window.
    His lunchbox in his hand, her back against the pole.

Dreams, he says he can see her, sitting in her rocking chair. when I turn out the lights. He wakes up screaming, most nights. It's hard on Mitch too, they have to share a room.
    Mrs B's lips are moving like a fish through the glass. No wonder he's exhausted in class.

Open, shut. Then open. His tummy is rumbling. He doesn't like fish.
    Luke?
    Please come here for a minute.

Sundays at Evelyn's: board games, chores, soccer in the park downstairs with Mitch. Evelyn makes pancakes while they tidy their bedroom. Three shelves and a large drawer have been cleared out for him. She'll fetch the rest of his clothes next week. Once she's been given the key for upstairs.
    He doesn't have to be afraid of the dark. He isn't. She only leaves the passage light on in case he needs the toilet. But ghosts do hide in cupboards. He read it in a book, from the school library.
    Mitch is going to stay at his dad for a few days.

The following weekend, Evelyn wakes them early. She's already packed a bag, snacks for their outing. Two hours later: ice cream, gulls, guitars, an empty hat held out in front of him. A mime in blue body paint with yellow hands. Mitch grabbing his arm to keep up.

Through the market, crowds, beside the ruins of settler cottages until they exit on a steep hill beside concrete railings and make their way to the foot of the Harbour Bridge.

Up stone steps that curve like a blackened nail, till they cup their hands over their foreheads and blink into the morning sun. Jagged, tree-patterned, the rough hem of the shoreline.

White specks, paper sailboats on turquoise cardboard and rocky edges, frayed and smoothed by the tide. Grey steel wedges docked at Garden Island and behind, the mast of a tall ship, obscured by ropes, sails.

Looking up, at the concrete spider webs, accessed by a lift. Small flakes of rust sticking to their palms, until they reach the viewing platform and Evelyn takes turns lifting the boys, to squint through the mesh into the winter sun and trace the watery loops of the Manly ferry with their fingertips. The boys sitting, cross-legged, tired, on concrete. Reaching into her backpack, before they rise, to be pushed along by Evelyn, and the ebbing crowd, deeper into the mouth of the bridge.

Mitch's dad will fetch him from school tomorrow.

Evelyn is going to get the keys to Luke's apartment.

There's a roll of thick garbage bags with yellow handles, in the kitchen drawer beside the stove. A bad smell from the cupboards. She will have to make several trips, most of the food has gone off. But other than Luke's room, there's not much to take. Like hers, their flat came furnished.

Some birthday gifts, a wooden train set, school books from the shelf behind his bed, his backpack, baseball—seven years, folded into one suitcase.

Evelyn is on her second trip up, when she sees it—her friend's rocking chair. Covered by a sheet beside the windowpane. The shape of the stand visible through the cotton, bunched and tucked into the rods at the back.

She reaches for the arms, the wavy patterns in the wood, like stick-carved curves in sand. Birch, or was it just plywood? Two bars on either side of the chair, like candlesticks with chunky rings, below the rounded torso. A cream pillow insert. Cotton threads, curling like hair ribbons. Five wooden bars at the back. Third bar from the right missing, but still seems solid.

Evelyn had found the rocking chair for her when Luke was just a few days old. Dumped, behind a mattress and base, blocking the corner of the pavement.

She's wrapping her arms around the chair, lifting the sheet, untucking the back. It needs some oil on the slats.

She's watching her friend as she sits, slowly, closing her eyes, pulling Luke towards her. The rocking motion soothing him, only an intermittent squeak. She can rest her arms now and still support him, his head leaning into her chest. Her feet against the slats, blanket around her shoulders, lulling them both to sleep.

You rest. I should go. I'll be back on the weekend.

When Evelyn returns, Luke is asleep on her lap.

Then they're in the kitchen, crouched on the tiles, beside sandpaper, spray, cloths. Turning the chair on its side, smoothing out splinters.

Mid-morning, lunchtime, afternoon naps, then three times or at best, twice a night, when he wakes. She couldn't have managed without the chair.

Her nipples are sore, Luke's having a growth spurt. His breathing is strained, his forehead burns against her palm.

Evelyn is standing by the window. Put a wet cloth on him. Or a lukewarm bath facing them.

She leans back, sighs, rocking until Luke settles again. He's asleep before she rises from the chair, adjusting his muslin wrap, gently lifting him over the bars, on the way to the front door.

Like the floor, the rocking chair is dusty.

Evelyn places a sheet on top, then sits down slowly. Her hands stretching behind her back, to the indented wooden grove on the left hand side of the chair, to the missing bar that they never replaced.

Evelyn sits in her friend's chair, Luke's chair. Rocking slowly, then faster, pulling her knees to her chest, blowing her nose, salt above her top lip, trickling towards her ears.

Slipping off her shoes, gripping the wood with her soles, backwards and forwards until the window frame blurs and she closes her eyes.

She stays, until the landlord's voice carries through the open front door and she slips on her sandals, feels for the keys and begins to drag the chair across the scuffed floorboards, towards the stairs.

The rocking chair fits inside Mitch's room, just. Though Mitch might not see it the way she does when he gets back from school. Beside the boys' window, behind Luke's mattress, until she works out what to do with it.

After school, Luke ignores the open suitcase on his mattress and runs towards the rocking chair. He is bending beside it, feeling the sides, a salty taste beneath his tongue, standing close to it, small drops like glass, falling from his eyes, onto his cheeks, the hairs on his arms, above his wrist, then finally, he's sitting, in his mum's rocking chair, their chair, his chair.

Evelyn relents. She lets him have his after-school milk and sandwich in the chair, instead of at the kitchen counter with Mitch, who threatens to dump the chair in Evelyn's bedroom, or on the street, when they are sleeping.

But Luke will only do his readers and his maths homework if he's sitting in the chair. He barely eats unless the plate is on his lap, his arms resting against the wood. Every day, for three weeks, he sits in the chair, she finds him there before the alarm clock rings for school and once, when she gets up for a glass of water in the middle of the night.

He won't go to the bathroom without making Mitch swear not to touch it. Why would he want to anyway? It's a piece of junk, it will give him splinters and he nearly tripped on it, when he leant over to open the blinds.

Why can't he move it out of their bedroom, there's space in the passage?

Evelyn is shaking her head, holding Mitch's hand, closing the balcony door, whispering to her son. Luke is watching them from the chair, through the half-opened bedroom door. Bubble words on their lips through the glass. Mitch's arms are crossed, Evelyn is squeezing his hand, hugging him, he's a good boy.

Then lifting her gaze towards Luke. Their eyes meet, he buries his face in the silhouette of the chair. She's back inside the kitchen, the front door is closing. Mitch, please wear your helmet, and come back upstairs in time for dinner.

Evelyn is walking towards their bedroom, leaning over him, her hand against the back of the rocking chair.

It's all right, Luke. You can keep the chair, in here I mean.

PE is on a Friday. Sometimes Luke leaves his bag behind on purpose. Mr Gibson shakes his head but says nothing. Luke prefers to sit in the bleachers, watching the star jumps, the skips, the laughter when a shoelace or plait catches the rope. The swapping of fruit from labelled containers, while the other boys help to pack the equipment away into a mesh bucket.

In assembly, every second Tuesday, he sits in the front, by himself, close to the stage, turning back every few minutes to watch Mrs B hush the mid-morning chatter, before the principal steps up to the lectern.

It's late spring, the jacaranda flowers begin to re-grow. By early summer the trees are in full bloom, the footpath to the front door of their building is slippery, blanketed in blossoms. He'll be seven in a few days time. His first birthday without her.

Mrs B always arranges a small class party.

Evelyn will bake a cake for him to bring in. He only likes Mum's chocolate cake, but he'll try it.

In circle time they are learning about adjectives to make their sentences more interesting. Then twos and fives and tens, number patterns till recess. There's a small spider in the frame of the windowsill behind his chair bag; he could catch it if he could find a small box. Odd numbers, even numbers, two digit numbers on the whiteboard in order, from greatest to least. But when he looks back, the spider is not there. Mrs B has coloured spinners on her desk, she wants the class to count them in groups of ten. The spider might have crawled into his chair bag. Or maybe it's dead, squished under his shoe.

They have to concentrate, otherwise they won't be able to bring in a toy next week, for show and tell.

It's Friday afternoon, they're walking home from school, slowly, chatting, pausing at the yellow castle. Evelyn wants to take them to the zoo, on his birthday. He's nodding, Mum taught him a lot about animals, do they have elephants? Mitch is on her left, Luke on her right. The tree by the entrance is in full bloom. The ground is damp, purple. She's stopped beside a low branch, they're watching her touch the branches as she talks. Each leaf is made up of hundreds of tiny leaflets.

Upstairs, she's cleaning the counter, boiling some water on the stove. She's going to make a special dinner, something Luke hasn't tried before. Mitch is on his bed with his headphones. She bought a small parsley plant. Luke is fetching her some leaves from the balcony. She's chopping vegetables, bending over the pot, the stalks in her palm, barely noticing when the doorbell rings. She hurries over in her apron, stiffening against the frame. He can hear voices, Evelyn is taking fast, in short bursts. When he looks up, there's a woman he recognises, an outline against the glass.

Tiger's Eye. She doesn't ask, she just closes the door to the bedroom and sits down, in his rocking chair. She is holding a notebook and a maroon folder, brushing away a jacaranda petal stuck to her handbag. She talks slowly. Something is making him cough. Evelyn is still holding the parsley leaves.

He must be feeling very sad, losing his mother, Evelyn has been so kind, but she's not his mother, he knows that, she is going to come back in the morning, to fetch him. He needs to pack all his clothes, his toys, tonight.

Evelyn will help him, the rocking chair is very special, she can tell, but it's too big to take with him.

Evelyn can visit him, often, Mitch too.

His throat tickles. By the time the spaghetti is cooked, the woman with the glasses is gone.

The purple-blue petals that stuck to her shoes have stained the entrance mat. In the passageway outside their apartment, another row of fallen leaves, dragged up the stairs under-heel and deposited on the carpet.

Mitch is leaning against the bed, Luke is still rocking in the chair, by the window. Evelyn is coming in and out of their room. She's crying, but she won't sit down. She's found an old suitcase from her top cupboard, she's packing his clothes into it. Folding his school shirts in neat rows, tucking his socks into the gaps beside his pyjamas, his school trousers. He's banging the chair against the floorboards.

She's coming over, putting her hand on the back of the chair, slowing him down, bending to hug him. She can't stop the woman, but it's going to be ok, it's not going to be for long. In the meantime, she's going to visit him, with Mitch, every weekend, if they can.

He's got to be brave. Mrs B is so proud of him, so is she, and Mitch, his friends and most of all, his mum. He's talented, and smart, his mum is watching over him, every single day. She's going with him too, in his heart.

He's gripping the sides of the chair tighter, he mustn't hurt himself, she understands if he wants to sit there, for a little longer. She's going to look after the chair for him too, until he comes back, she won't let anyone sit in it, not even Mitch, in case it breaks. She knows his mum would not like it to break. He doesn't want food, she'll bring a tray, next to his bed, with a sandwich, in case he gets hungry in the night. She's coming back at 8 a.m. He's got to stay calm, it's ok to cry, it's ok to feel scared, but he's got to be calm, and remember how much everyone loves him. It's only going to be for a little while, till she gets everything sorted out, she'll talk to Mrs B, and his friends, to let them know it's only for a bit, and she'll ask Mrs B to give Little Cat a big hug for him.

It's almost midnight, she's kissed him goodnight, and hugged him, and kissed him goodnight again, she's walking backwards, turning off the lamp, Mitch is fast asleep in his bed, Luke's still in the rocking chair, he can't be too loud, on the floorboards, because of the neighbours, but he can stay there, in the chair, if he wants to, tonight, he's not going to bed. She won't sleep either, but she's going to rest. He's rocking slowly, trying not to scrape the back of the chair against the bed.

His eyes are starting to close, he's got to stay awake, he can't let them, he's opening the curtains, the moon is narrow, halved, there are no clouds, but there are stars, he can see the yellow tips of the castle, the tower reflected under them, except he was wrong, it's not a castle, it's a rubbish dump, or whatever it was, where they took rubbish away, Evelyn told Mitch, Mitch told him, it was where they burned it, in the big tower, it used to be bigger, in the smoke, the flames, the light, the tower seems taller now through the glass, he can feel the heat of the rubbish burning, he can smell it, through the window, it's stinky and smoky, it's making his eyes water, then he's asleep, his hand still holding the curtain …

The summer carpet of violet-blue flowers has passed, the asphalt is bare. The jacaranda leaves have turned yellow and dropped, there's no shade from the thinning foliage.

The winter rains are heavy, the soil is like wet clay.

The Department turns down Evelyn's application, the reasons are unclear. She passes all the background checks to foster, she answers their questions well in the interview. She doesn't have a spare bedroom, that's true, but she can't afford to rent a three bed. The boys are like brothers, they're used to sharing.

She's known him since he was born, she promised his mother. Their responses are short, sharp, the language is generic. Regrettably, she's not a suitable person, they need to act in Luke's best interests, for the long term. The case worker will be in touch in the coming months, to discuss the contact arrangements.

The gully behind Evelyn's building overflows, the wheels of parked vehicles are submerged. Rain pools at the edges of the road and flows like an open drain, under cars, towards the creek (once swamp and marshland). The water is sludge and swamp wattle, centuries of wool washing, dairies, brickworks and glass, industrial waste soaked into pebbles, algae and sedge. Small frogs and birds swoop low for fish or perch on the small overhanging bridge.

Evelyn can barely get out of bed, grief knots around her like a branch. It's not Mitch's fault, she has to be there for him too. If she reacts or complains every time they ignore her emails, her phone calls, when they 'forget' to tell her that Luke's moved again, or which school he's attending, they'll say she's a troublemaker, they'll tell her even less, harden their position.

The air is moist and heavy, thick grey cloth. The contact arrangements Evelyn proposes are rejected by the Department.

There's a lot for them to consider. The social worker has a lot of observations. About his needs, his trajectory. It unsettles him, she says, when Evelyn visits. They know she's upset and they are trying to keep her informed. Things can change, quickly sometimes, where he's staying, for instance. They have to respond in the moment, but they're short-staffed and they can only brief her when they have time. She's not his parent or his guardian. They need to focus on Luke.

The rains have delayed the jacarandas, spring is cold, the new buds are late to bloom.

Mitch is sitting beside Evelyn's bed holding her hand. She can't give up. She's got to fight.

The following day, she withdraws her savings and pays for legal advice. They request a mediation with the Department on her behalf. She has to make her case, why she should have frequent contact, given that she's not his legal guardian.

They explain nothing. The mediator is not on her side, but he's supposed to be neutral. She watches his shoes, entering, re-entering, opening another door. She's there all day, the case worker and her cannot see eye to eye.

She needs legal representation. Luke's moving so often, they've stopped telling her.

She takes out a loan and goes to court, to seek orders. The magistrate rules in the Department's favour.

They won't give her any more credit. She sells her car to pay the lawyer's bill.

They bloom eventually, in late summer, weaving their floral archways over the streets. Dream trees, majestic lavender, mauve, electric blue. Leaves like lush ferns, feeding on sun and light. Soft canopies of fragrant, tubular petals. Drawing aphids, flies and scale. Leaf spot. Spider mites and mildew. Rotting inside its spreading, water-logged root system. Before the end of autumn—foliage thinning again, fading to butter-gold, shedding onto railings, suffocating fishponds and gutters, leaves falling like tears onto the paving.

seven years

The morning sky is flat, a smooth grey pebble.

There's a row of trees across from the house where the social worker's car has stopped, the limbs are pitted and knotty, the bark is brown and grey. The roots jut out, like pointing toes.

Luke has been in a supervised hostel for five months, waiting for this placement. His scalp is itchy, he's got ringworm between his fingers. He lives in boxes, bags.

At the window of a bedroom, the family is still asleep. The pyjamas they gave him are too big. The blinds are broken, there's a sheet hanging over the window frame. He pulls the sheet to one side. The pavement is bathed in shadows, the trees bare, sloped. The bedroom is cold, he brings the blanket to wrap around him, tracing his palm along the frosted glass. Outside, cottages with high chimneys, low iron fences, sloping roofs. He's scratching his head. His nose against the glass, waiting for a possum or a cat roaming the light-flooded street, climbing cables, or asleep under a parked car.

The social worker is holding a roll of garbage bin liners, opening the cupboard, reaching for his clothes on the top shelf, throwing them inside. Outside, lavender bells on the branches cluster in panicles. The flowers have short floral stalks, the older ones grow close to the base. They don't have long; she has to drop him at the next placement before dark.

She's pulling the bags down the stairs, into the backseat of the car, there is no one downstairs when they leave. His scalp is so itchy. He doesn't ask where they're going.

His new school is on a hill, once a quarry, the wall is like a compound, the pavement slopes, there's an overhanging bridge adjoining both sides of the school grounds. The boys wait in clusters behind the bathrooms. There's blood on his collar, the other boy got detention, he got off with a warning.

His head is still aching when the bell wails. Velcro, buckles, raised heels crowding the gravel path to the school gate.

At the new home, he can hear the TV through the bedroom door, a man is asleep on the couch. In the street behind the house there's a concrete fence, a highway on the other side. The school nurse says he has lice. The carer takes him to get his head shaved.

He closes his eyes, tyres are striking the pavement, goods trucks, petrol tankers heading down the coast, diesel, rubber on asphalt, rolling, speeding, braking along the bending and paving, engines, exhausts, fumes from the chimney stacks along the spine of the junction, once a railway yard.

The smoke is tickling his throat, his nostrils, he closes the glass frame, he tries but he just can't stop coughing, then he can hear voices, a fist against his wall, the door opens, the TV man is holding his slipper in his hand.

The school has no heating in winter and it boils in late summer. He's chewing his nails, shivering, seated at the front of the empty classroom, his back to the board. Facing rows of plastic chairs, their metallic legs tucked beneath tables. Closed windows, a fluorescent glare.

The small jacaranda tree outside his classroom is bare, its limbs coated in frost.

After dinner, the new family watch game shows. He's clearing the table, carrying their plates through to the kitchen. He trips on the rug along the passageway. A mug shatters on the tiles, the handle still attached. The remainder in small shards and splinters on the tray beside him. He's a clumsy piece of shit. The man stops watching TV and comes towards him, bending down with his cigarette. Then he's yelping, holding his upper arm, a perfectly round circle, smoke rising from his burnt skin. Slamming the door, turning up the volume, laughing.

He starts to see them in his dreams at night, disfigured, he wakes up with an outline of sweat traced into his pillow cover.

Mostly it's his mum—sitting, while he stands close to the feet of her chair, his arms raised, leaning forward, waiting to be lifted and folded into her lap. But she doesn't speak, she turns away, then she's lying on a bed with a wet cloth against her back, she is ill, he's in the bathroom looking for her medicine, he can't reach the cabinet, he's standing on the edge of the bath, now he's running back to her, but her eyes are hollow, her clothes are in a pile at his feet.

He's pleading with her to open her mouth, to sit up, to swallow the medicine, but her lips are closed, she's pulling the blanket over her face. He lifts the blanket to rest the face cloth against her burning forehead, but she is on the floor, facedown, dissolving like mist.

He begs them to keep the bathroom light on, but the TV man won't.

When the family is out in the afternoon, he sits on the couch trying to work the TV remote. Beside the coffee table, there's a plant. The sun pours through the window, the leaves look large and glossy. But when he leans closer, there are no veins, the leaves are flat and don't bend. Small bits of plastic peel off the tips like stickers in his hands.

There are no brown spots or splits in the leaves, the undersides are all luminous green. The midrib in the centre feels like a rubber toy, the stems droop, the leaves are like stamps, the stems—plastic ribbon. Polyester, nylon, vinyl, they're rough on his fingertips. Polyethylene, dye. The colour is the same from branch to twig.

A few of the moulded leaves have detached and have fallen beside the pot, gathering dust. He picks up one, it has a strange chemical smell. Carbon dioxide, petroleum. The plant has no breath, soil, water. Mid-afternoon light coats the artificial leaves but doesn't filter through. Plastic, iron.

They move him, eventually, but only after a teacher asks about his arm, and the bruising behind his legs.

They're pulling into a driveway, it's already dark, he can't make out anything, except the frame of the house and the roof. The social worker is piling the garbage bags on the front porch, a woman is coming to the door, he can hear a baby crying inside the house, she's gesturing to him, come inside.

There's a long passageway, between the upstairs bedrooms, there are five other kids staying too, he'll meet them later. She can't put the baby down, it's supposed to be naptime but he's got colic, he's not settling. There's some cold pasta in the fridge. She's walking back up the stairs, the baby is still staring at him.

The other boys come out of their bedrooms to watch him pull his plastic bags along the corridor. They're leaning against the doorframes, they're all brothers or cousins. They look similar.

He's asleep in his room, blanket pulled up to his neck.

Suddenly there's a weight pressing down on his chest, he can't inhale, his muscles are contracting, he's gasping trying to sit up, he can hear laughter, the older brother or the cousin is rolling off him, onto the floor, the other two are waiting, hysterical, high-fiving him, as he runs towards them, slamming the door behind them.

The next morning is warmer, the carer asks him to sit with her and the baby in the small garden. It's late spring, the jacaranda leaves are re-growing. Still yellow-brown, waiting for the first flowerings of summer. The bark is brittle and scaly. Along the midrib, suspended from a swaying branch—long leaflets, each with a cluster of smaller leaflets. There are gaps along the rows of smaller leaflets, from winter, dehydration. The old seed pods will ripen with the new flowers.

He shouldn't worry, they're like this with all the new kids.

She lowers her arms, the baby crawls away, towards the pot plants, the woman following behind to pick the small pebbles out of the way.

The carer's eyes are kind, she takes him to buy new clothes. The baby sleeps in the pram while he tries on a school shirt in the change room. He's allowed to play video games after homework (though the other boys hardly let him).

He dreams about Mum, Evelyn and him, folding his clothes into a bag, leaning against the kitchen cupboard while the kettle boils, or reading to him while Mitch is asleep on the sofa. Then he's lying in the grass, he's fallen off his bicycle, Evelyn is running towards him, holding a bag of ice against his elbow, the ice is wetting the sleeve of his flannel shirt, his mum is rolling it up, then picking him up in her arms, kissing his open palm.

He wakes up around midnight, the lights in the passage are off. The doors to the other bedrooms are closed, he can see the outline of the small garden in the reflection of the streetlights. He's about to get back into bed when he catches sight of a tail, wrapped around a bar in the gate, something jumping onto a large round pot plant, then two sets of eyes illuminating, orange-gold in the dark garden—a baby possum on its mother's back, circling the rim of the plant, then climbing between the low branches, burrowing in the pebbly soil, chewing the leaves, jumping to another smaller plant, then back again. They're scaling the garden fence, disappearing outside.

In the morning light, brown pellets litter the verandah. The soil smells like wee. There are holes in the leaves of the pot plants, the new buds have been broken off. The carer sweeps the possum droppings with a large broom, but they are back again the next morning, and the next.

She won't let her baby into the garden until she's swept the tiles. The husband trims the branches of the trees and covers the drains. She soaks the base of the plants in peppermint oil but they come back night after night. She peels garlic cloves, soaking them for hours in boiling water. The cloves take on a blue tinge and float to the top. When the mixture cools, she uses a funnel to pour it into a plastic spray bottle, coating the remaining leaves every morning.

But the holes get bigger, the last leaves are disappearing, she sweeps daily but the dried droppings collect along the edges of the verandah and beneath the door frames. She buys a portable sensor light and leaves it on the garden chair. The fluorescent light from the garden floods the edges of Luke's bedroom window, waking him intermittently.

There are fewer now but the droppings still appear. They're there, every morning, when she opens the sliding doors.

On humid summer afternoons, she turns on the sprinklers and they fight for a turn to run through the spray. The carer goes inside with the baby to fetch them hats. He is lying in the grass, soaking his feet in a bucket. There's no shade. The leaves sting like sunburn on his fingertips, the tree bark is scalding.

By early evening, it's cooler. He sits in the kitchen with her while she feeds the baby, passing her a cloth from the sink to wipe the high chair.

The other boys hide bugs or sometimes dead snails under his blanket, he'll find some stones in the garden. The baby's chin is covered in porridge, she wants to know if he has any siblings. The baby laughs when he pulls out his tongue or pretends to hide behind the chair.

The garlic cloves sink, the mixture in the spray bottle smells sour like vinegar, the droppings appear on the tiles every morning.

When he returns from school, all of the pot plants are gone, the husband is in the driveway, piling them onto the back of his ute to take to the dump. There are no droppings the next morning, the garden is bare in the early light.

A few weeks later, the carer is driving the baby to daycare when the bell rings. The husband opens the front door.

It's the social worker, calling upstairs to Luke, holding another roll of bin bags.

Luke's new foster home is next to a warehouse, there are five kids, two of their own.

He's sharing a room with two other boys, his new carer doesn't talk to him, there are meals, but mostly they just find things in the cupboards when they're hungry.

They don't have a spare uniform for him, but he follows the others to school anyway.

There's a concrete factory at the end of the road—sand and gravel, cement. The older boys run ahead, he watches the reversing trucks through the fence, tanks and nozzles, pipes, conveyor belts. Shafts, mixers, feeders, pumps and bins, mixing the dry, then dispatching, water run-off and sludge into the creek behind the factory.

Dried leaves and stalks clump the sloping gutters, blocking the downpipes. Rain cascades over the edge of the roof. He needs a jacket, but the carer is shaking her head. His clothing allowance hasn't arrived. He showers late at night, when the bathroom is free. When he comes out of the bathroom, his backpack is open, his belongings are on the floor, the other boys are pretending to snore.

The foster carer is holding the door handle, there's someone here to see him.

It's the first time they've spoken in months. Evelyn is hugging him. Luke can hear the other boys crouched outside the bedroom door listening. They're both crying. They've have stolen his things, the carer thinks he's lying, but he's not, they're punishing him, they hate him. She can hear the panic rising in his voice, he can defend himself, but he needs her to take him out of here, he needs to see Mitch. She's holding his hand, she's trying, she's fighting for him every day, but in the meantime, he's got to stay strong, he can't let them win.

The contact visit is over before lunchtime, the carer only lets him walk Evelyn to the front door.

The air is biting, he can make out the top of the cement silos that lead down to the conveyer belts, the shafts and chutes. Silica, fly ash, solvent. He's gripping Evelyn's arm but the carer is calling him back inside.

He can smell concrete dust from the mixers inside his nostrils.

After Evelyn leaves he climbs into the bottom bunk and falls asleep. In his dream, Tiger's Eye is back for him, he's burying his face in his mum's rocking chair, his thumb in his mouth, legs folded. The wooden bar at the back of the chair is missing, another one is loose. He lifts his head, stands, faces her, she's laughing, holding the missing piece of wood above his head.

He's on his knees like a toddler, Tiger's Eye is closing her fingers around the column of wood, pulling it towards him, closer. Then she's gone but now the TV man is crouching over him, until there is a snap and a sharp pain below his fingertips, then he's awake, battling to catch his breath.

Luke's in the stairwell, waiting outside another apartment. It's on the eighth floor, the lift is broken. He's waiting for the new couple to stop fighting.

The cladding outside the building runs vertically, in strips, between the balconies, the upright panel like a wooden ruler. It's just him and the couple.

There are twelve floors in the building. Outside—a small car park, a fence, the curved neck of a street lamp and beside it, a large tree. The leaves drape like a necklace over the bark, feathery, pale green.

He can hear things being thrown inside.

At night the couple lock the balcony door, but through the glass he can see the city, stretching like a long spine, rows of stone and concrete, buildings stacked in neat rows, fused against train tracks, old tram lines, a glimpse of water, the late-night ferry crossing the harbour.

There's a different social worker, driving Luke to his new placement. She doesn't talk, he doesn't ask questions. His clothes are on the backseat, in sealed plastic bags.

The new home is over the bridge.

Across the harbour—a large ferris wheel rotating slowly, pausing, resuming. Small boats, rolling side to side, sails opening, water like frothy milky. She can't come inside, but they're expecting him.

The new house is narrow, long, dark in the middle of the day, with an iron-rim verandah and a wide front garden.

The bedroom is large, he doesn't have to share. It's a two-storey terrace, four bedrooms but just the two of them. Her name is Magda, she's old, her husband is dead. There are papers piled up behind an armchair, a briefcase, golf clubs beside the front door and in the armchair in the study downstairs, curled up with its tail over its face—a small tabby.

He can hear her in the passage talking to herself, or the cat.

There's a tray on his desk, next to some textbooks, for his new school. A long passageway runs between the kitchen and the lounge. His feet echo on the parquet flooring.

The bathroom walls are tiled, the water runs cloudy for a few seconds when he turns on the tap. He's standing beside the basin, she's given him an old pair of socks.

Through the gap underneath the door, he can see a tail brush past, he opens it, but the cat is already halfway down the stairs.

Across the street, there's a small park. He's in bed, he can't sleep. It's the jacaranda pods, brittle, rattling, falling, with a small clang, outside his window, over, again.

There are other children in his dreams, ones he's met, still to meet.

Crowded around him, beside a lamp in an unfamiliar bedroom, asking him questions. Then a door opening, a hiss, a scuffle, silence, something knocking his elbow, then he's falling, falling from the top of a bunk bed.

Sometimes Mrs B, his old teacher, is in his dreams, but she won't look him in the eye—he's misplaced Little Cat, he was only meant to have her for a couple of days, as a reward for being good in class, but now she's lost too.

Or, he's in another home, with the TV man who is passing him a pile of plates that slip out of his hands. He can feel them staring when he swallows.

Another new school, sandwiches on the steps behind the hall, lockers in the corridor. A cloth on the board, traces of whiteboard marker and fractions.

At lunchtime he crouches behind the stone building, collecting jacaranda pods. Flat, rounded discs, He snaps a pod open, the seeds feel papery, they spill onto his lap.

The school building used to be a convent. They pray every morning in the chapel, the bell tower still rings.

Behind the principal's desk—a row of bronze-rimmed and silver trophies. A large freckle where his knuckle joins his fingers.

He hit me first, Sir, I was just waiting in line.

The bells are hung in a frame, tied to the axle of a rotating wooden wheel. There's a rope tied to the spokes, running through the holes and pulleys. Hammers, louvres, slide, cage, headstock. The clapper hitting the inside, sounding as the rope pulls.

This is not the first time. The other boy's parents have laid a formal complaint. He can hear the bell, chiming outside the principal's' window.

Beneath his bedroom door—pools of light from the bathroom. There's the gap in the blinds, a slatted finger, bunched and twisted beside the cords. His elbow knocks against the bedside table.

The carer's door is still closed, he can hear her snoring; he tiptoes downstairs to find the cat.

There are newspapers discarded beside a desk. The windowpanes slice the morning sun. The armchair in the study is cushioned with ball and claw feet, the leather is starting to fade. The upper curves of its legs bow outwards, the lower concave.

The cat is curled under the chair, its front paw bent forward against its nose, hugging its whiskers.

There are streaks of black and gold on its forehead, a small bald patch. He had seen it scratching yesterday above one eye.

He bends down gently, the cat rolls onto its back, the fur in front is longer, golden, its tummy has a kind of pouch, it's lifting its paws into the air.

He reaches to pat it, but the cat jumps forward, then away, onto the windowsill.

I will not use   fists   instead of   words
I will not use fistsinstead of words
I   willnotuse fists instead   of words
I will   not use fistsinstead ofwords
~~I willnot use fists instead of words~~

The school bell has rung for the day. Outside, play hats, Mary Janes, knee-high socks. Sports bags and day bags and keyrings, in piles beside the bus stop. Waiting for brothers or sisters to flood out of the school gates. They pretend to look away as he passes, their eyes, their laughter burning his back. He turns away.

The jacarandas are blooming, washing the pavement with foxglove flowers.

The cat is not allowed outside.

The carer gives him a bag of kibbles, but they the cat doesn't like to play with toys. Luke cuts long pieces of string and weaves them together and ties them to back of the kitchen chair.

The cat watches him, then circles the chair. Suddenly, the ends of the string are in its mouth, it's on its back paws swatting the string from side to side.

He wakes up early every morning to spend time with the cat before school.

The carer shows him how to brush its long fur, he shapes the clumpy piles of discarded hair into a ball, then rinses off the brush.

Its ears are itchy, the skin on either side is thin and flaking from scratching, Luke helps her to hold the cat while she puts in some eardrops.

He's pulling back the wisps of curtain lining, leaning against the glass, watching the street below. Blurred figures in the rain, crossing a road, pausing, quartered through the frame of the study window.

On the weekend the cat is sneezing, there's gunk coming out of its eyes. He goes with her to vet, his hand on its fur while the vet goes in and out of the door to the back of the clinic.

When he comes home from school a few days later, the social worker is waiting outside. He can see the cat watching him through the living room window.

It's been raining, there's a trail of small pebbles and squashed leaves, from the gate to the front door.

Magda has had a fall, she's in hospital.

He needs to pack his things. A neighbour will look after the cat.

In his dreams, they sit, on the mattress beside Mitch's bed, his knuckles still partly closed, his head against Evelyn's shoulder. She can read him another story. But it's his last night, there's no time. There's a gap behind the cushion, in the torso of his mum's chair, but it still rocks. Evelyn is turning the pages slowly, making rectangular shadows that crouch, then rise in the fluorescent glow. There are damp spots from the rain on the carpet of Mitch's room, the doorbell is ringing, he knows he has to go.

The door is barricaded, it doesn't lock, it's almost midnight.

His new foster carers are asleep. Their teenage son sleeps in the room next door. There are two other foster kids staying too. There are framed pictures of the son above on the piano. He twists Luke's arm and throws him towards the kitchen counter, while his mother is running errands.

When the new carer gets home, Luke is crying.

At dinner, she asks him about school, he presses his hand on the underside of the table. The wood is rough and splintery.

On Saturdays, they walk to the large park nearby, once a swamp, a forest of ironbarks, then a factory, brick-pits and the remnants of a rubbish dump, now decaying beneath the topsoil. The son throws the ball at his face, his cheek is starting to swell. The boys ignore him and carry on playing.

He sits with the carer on a bench beside the grassy wetland ponds, watching dogs chasing each other, a group of girls jumping stepping stones across the pond.

The new school has a tiny playground, they have to rotate lunch breaks to avoid overcrowding. There's no school bell, music plays over the loudspeaker to signal the end of lunch.

He comes down to breakfast in the school uniform they gave him, sitting opposite a new family. A woman is holding a box of cereal, carefully opening the cardboard box, pouring it into his bowl. One of the children passes him the milk, but his elbow accidentally knocks against the carton, spilling milk onto his school pants.

He's sitting on the rim of the toilet, shaking his head, crying. The front of the pants are soaked, from the waist to the knees, the children are going to laugh at him, say he's weed his pants. He can't go to the school like this, not until his pants are dry.

The carer is knocking on the bathroom door. They'll shrink in the tumble dryer, but he can use her hairdryer, on the damp bits, she'll wait downstairs.

The wet patches have faded by the time he comes downstairs, he says nothing on the walk to his new school.

His fingers are looped around the straps of his backpack, she waits with him at the entrance to the admin office, he looks straight ahead, she's introducing herself to the school receptionist, patting Luke on the shoulder when a teacher arrives to collect him.

He walks home after school, the carer wants to know about his first day. He can see her slippers, moving up and down, slightly, on the footrest below her desk. A group of boys locked him in the cubicles, they emptied his lunch into the toilet. Her voice is quieter. Her feet are pressing against the floor, he needs to make an effort to fit in.

Term days smudge together. One morning, the carer asks if he can stop at the shop on the way back from school, to buy some milk.

He can see cars reversing out of factories across the road.

After the bell rings, he takes the long route to the shop, around the park, so his shoes don't get dirty. The paper handle of the shopping bag is starting to tear from the weight, he grips his fingers tightly around the bag. In the park, he can see dogs circling their owners, running up and down the path between the trees.

He stops, leaning against a fence when he recognises the boy on the bicycle from school, another one from his class rides past, on a scooter.

The late afternoon sun is low, the leaves look glazed by the light that brushes through the branches and foliage.

The street glows in the reflection of car windows.

Luke squints into the horizon, his heel catches the paving as he crosses the road, he trips, landing in a pile of leaves and damp blue decaying petals beside the pavement.

He's standing up, brushing away the leaves stuck to the sides of his shoes. The plastic milk bottle is ok, but the shopping bag has ripped.

It's nearly dark when he returns. His eyes scan the front garden. The porch light is on. His trainers are dirty, unlaced and now stained purple under the soles of the shoes.

He's suspended by the end of the second week, even though he was defending himself, and he has a black eye. Next time will be longer, maybe they'll expel him.

The carer doesn't talk to him any more at breakfast, looking only towards her son. He presses his palms into the underside of the table. He can feel small splinters digging into his skin.

The son kicks him, in front of her. She says nothing, sitting back in her chair, adjusting the tablecloth.

After he's eaten, he runs upstairs again, locking the bedroom door.

He keeps the light on all night, he doesn't want to dream any more. His mum is waiting for him, but she's stuck to a chair, injured, bleeding. He kneels down to help her but he can't stop it. Congealing streaks run down the wooden legs of the chair, then the torso, arms, back, then the seat, the cushion. He looks up, his mum is gone, but there is dried blood on his shoes, on the floor beside her rocking chair.

The placement ends suddenly, a few days later. The social worker is there to collect him when he gets home from school, she's already started packing his clothes. The son is watching them from his bedroom window as she reverses the car.

He's in a new home, turning his bag upside down, emptying the contents onto the rug in the middle of the room. It was there, he knows he packed it, the framed picture of his mum, he saw it inside his bag in the social worker's car. In the picture, she sits. In her rocking chair, their chair, a small pillow tucked behind her, jutting out behind her elbow. Little Cat is on the shelf behind the chair, a row of his books, the window slightly open. Sun pouring through, the photo slightly overexposed.

He finds the frame eventually, in a smaller garbage bag, the edge has pierced a hole in the plastic.

His mum is smiling in the photo, her mouth open, he had made her laugh moments before. She had saved for months, putting the money aside from her salary every fortnight, the camera was his special birthday present. It was one of the first he took, his small hand still unsteady, the chair appearing slightly askew, the shelf at an angle, but she loved it, he was a natural.

She had bought a frame the next day. He watched her, carefully lifting out the glass, securing the cardboard backing, closing the hooks on each side of the frame slowly, with her nails, then placing it on the windowsill, beside their chair.

His nose is blocked, he's wailing loudly into the pillow, the carer is knocking on the door, he can't answer her.

He's pulling his knees to his chest, crying loudly, still holding the frame.

The carer comes in anyway. His face is against the pillow, his empty bag on the floor beside the bed.

He's sitting up, picking up the pillows, throwing them in her direction, shouting. She's standing up, her mouth open, backing away, closing his door.

Faces press against the door as they pass the classroom, the open-shut of the handle, muffled laughter.

Move along boys!

They're turning back anyway, sticking out their tongues, pulling faces at Luke through the glass.

He is stuck in detention until the end of the day. He doesn't have a jumper, there are goosebumps on the back of his knees. Knock like this, if you need to go to the toilet. It's an opportunity to reflect. He can hear the PE teacher's whistle. The boys are lining up on the field. Again. The sound carries through the open window, a sharp shrill cry. His can feel himself wheezing when he inhales.

He's been here for hours, his mouth is dry, he's hungry, he needs to pee. He's standing up, banging on his desk. There's a pile of chairs at the back of the classroom, tall and neatly stacked. He climbs onto a desk and reaches for the top chair, throwing it, then another. Metal legs smack the rubber flooring. The rubber muffles the sound. There are only a few left now, he throws the last one on the floor, jumping down from the desk.

It's the end of the day but the school bell is broken. The classroom is silent, littered with plastic chairs, on their sides, their backs, their fronts. There are a couple in front of the storeroom, he's reaching for those too, there's a chair in his arms, above his head, when the teacher opens the door.

The carer's husband is standing beside him, throwing his textbooks, shoes, water bottle, slamming his lunchbox onto the floor beside his schoolbag, holding the principal's note in his hand.

The neighbours can probably hear them. TV is banned, he's got to fix his attitude and earn his keep.

They're disappointed, no—ashamed. He's wasting every chance he's given.

Luke keeps his eyes fixed on the tablecloth. The husband's back is pressed against the dining room chair, his feet are clenched against the legs of the table.

He's grounded.

Wake, shower, walk, bell, lessons.
Lunch, lessons, bell, walk, dinner.

He pretends to be sick the next morning. He can hear the school bell in his dreams.

The new foster family has a fourteen-year-old daughter, Luke is turning fifteen soon.

The husband shouts from the other room. They're at the table close to the stove, eating lamb and vegetables. The daughter looks past him, at the clock on the wall.

On the bookshelf beside the kitchen counter, there are recipe books and an ashtray shaped like a dog. His elbows are on the table, the knife and fork still where he set them. It's polite to answer people when they ask you something. The vegetables are still on his plate. The carer is starting to wash up, the daughter is watching him. When he looks up, her eyes are blank, empty. He can see the outline of branches through the window, swaying, clenched, like a closing fist.

There is spare soap in the cupboard under the sink, bath towels, face cloths on his bed, the switch for the bedside lamp is behind the table. He can hear her whispering in the daughter's room, as he walks through the passage.

It's not on purpose, but the woman's porcelain ashtray is in his hand, broken, with a large crack between the tail and the body of the dog. It's after school. She'll be back shortly, from the shops. The daughter walks into the kitchen. He puts his hands behind his back, but there are shards of cracked porcelain beside him on the floor.

He's in the social worker's car again. The radio is on, cockatoos are balancing on electrical wires above the street. There's a new house, large, old, across the road from the train station.

The street is sloped, bathed in jacaranda leaves. He's been in eighteen different homes, it's almost his birthday again. The social worker is angry he keeps getting suspended. She's opening the boot, passing him the bag. She won't meet his eyes.

The branches are bent fingers, stretching over the station wall. The ground is like a billowing dress, damp violet-blue ruffles and decaying leaves fall onto the train lines, mixing with gravel, crushed stone. Sharp rock ballast—cinders, clay, sand—draining water, anchoring the tracks.

Graffiti covers the low wall that separates the street from the station. At night, the train screeches like a school bell, hissing as it slows to a stop.

They can hear the train through the windows of the dining room. He looks down when the man addresses him.

His wife is turning off the oven. Juice spills over his plate, onto the tablecloth. It was an accident. The man moves closer to Luke, growling, his fist banging the table. Luke's tongue feels frozen, the man's arm is above his neck, he's shaking his head, apologising, sinking lower in his chair.

The man is coming closer towards him. Luke's pants feel warm, suddenly, and the man can see it too. There's a wet patch forming on the chair, the man is backing away, shouting. He's disgusting, filth. His wife is at the door, he's grabbing the cloth from her hands, throwing it at Luke, here, he'd better clean up his own piss.

He falls asleep listening for the train, headlights, high voltage cables. Marker lights, windscreen wipers, hinged doors.

He dreams of Mum, wrapped in folds of material, blankets are covering her hands. Luke is sitting and on the floor beside her, next to a pair of shoes. His mum is leaning forwards, the curved legs of the chair against her heels. The upholstery is dusty, her back is pressed against the dark red folds of the chair, her ankles against its clawed feet. They're his shoes, but they look different. They're polished, leather, with small holes beside the laces. He pauses, then turns away to put them on. Standing up, but he gets up too quickly. The boot crushes her bare foot, she's screaming. He's hugging her, crying, then the chair is empty. There's a funny taste in his mouth, like blood.

The pedestrian crossing leads to a footbridge. Dried flowers and leaves accumulate on the bridge and the stairs, on the signage, pooling on the canopies over the platforms. There's a ramp from the underpass, a lift down to the concourse, bicycle racks, CCTV cameras.

The neighbour's dog barks when the train is near. The carer's husband beats him with a belt.

He can see the station flickering through the curtains, the emergency light stays on all night.

Luke leaves early for school, the husband is not downstairs yet.

He hasn't spoken to Evelyn since his last placement, she had cried the whole visit, he doesn't want her to see him here.

He follows the train tracks, down the steep hill of leaves and damp petals, under a low bridge towards the school. The bell rings for the first period as he arrives at the gate.

The train calls him, with a cry or a low hum, on the way to school, or on the journey home. It reminds him of Evelyn, his mum. He learns the routing and the schedule off by heart, from a leaflet that he found on the ground, beside the turnstiles.

In the dark, he counts hours in night trains, the rhythms of wheels on crushed gravel, the driver slowing, releasing the brakes, or accelerating as he leaves the station behind him.

He listens for the weekend crowds, leaving clusters of litter behind the benches, pushing their way into a crowded train.

One Saturday night, he is woken by wailing, flashing, police cars parked across from the house. The street is awake, lit with sirens.

A man has fallen onto the train tracks, neighbours pour from their houses to watch. The carer's husband is swearing, slamming the bedroom door, his wife is in her dressing gown on the front porch.

Luke watches from his bedroom window, hours pass, then he can see them finally, emerging from the station, a body covered on a stretcher, closing the ambulance doors.

Thinning trees curve into the shoulder of the station. Small aphids line the tips of the leaves. Purple blooms, in clusters around the trunks, flakes of broken bark, leaves and debris collect on the pavement.

Luke pretends to join the rush hour crowds as he makes his way across the footbridge every morning.

Tracks, signals, currents, electrified wires overhead. His new school is one block from the station. On the sports field, he watches trains slip away from the platforms.

Through the glass, foam seats, like rows of blue petals.

He studies the timetable and reads the names of the stations aloud when they're out.

From the early morning, running every fifteen minutes, more frequently at rush hours, slowing during the day, stopping around midnight.

The train map loops in lines and coloured swirls. Horizontal and diagonal limbs like small branches and twigs or woody stems bearing new buds, bringing water to the leaves.

The husband beats him with a different belt strap.

Violet-blue blossoms that dressed the trees have fallen like clumps of hair, onto windscreens and front gates, sticking to the soles of his school shoes, decomposing on pavements and letter boxes. The bark is full of tiny specks.

On the way to school, he picks up a few pods that have fallen onto the path. An elderly woman in the house next door waves to him as she sweeps flowers with a plastic broom. He knows it has to be tonight.

After school, Luke packs all his belongings into a duffel bag and hides it under the bed. The afternoon stretches like a long, cylindrical train. Points, crossovers, signal boxes, underground links, main western, southern, north, coast, airports, parks, city, goods lines, or trams, on viaducts, cuttings, above-ground, stub tunnels, disused, road bridges, corridors.

He's at dinner, passing a bowl of spaghetti to the husband, a globe above the table has gone out.

He can hear the carer saying something. She is sitting next to him but her voice is muffled, the man is shaking his head.

Luke's hand is shaking.

Through the window, the headlights of the approaching train, watching him from the darkened street, like cat-eyes shining red, glowing yellow, reflecting the moon, scattering stars.

He studies the train map to stay awake.

He can hear dishes being stacked, the dryer on another cycle, the husband turning off the TV, pipes squeaking through his bedroom wall from the shower, possums in the overhead ceiling.

The house is single-storey, red brick. His bedroom is next to the bathroom, there's mould along the skirting boards beside his bed, his door is swollen, the handle sticks and creaks when he opens it.

He waits for the last train before midnight. He can hear the husband snoring through the wall when he opens the bedroom window, crouching through the gap, lowering himself down, pulling his duffel bag behind him, a small jump over the ledge, bones, muscles, tendons landing softly on the grass beside the fence.

He crosses the street.

Branches scratch the wall beside the train tracks, crossing over each other, moving, shrinking, cracking along the trunk, where aphids have dug holes into the bark, flaking wood into strips on the pavement, the wind whispering into the cracks of roofs, wrapping itself around stems and drying leaves.

In the silent station, rain pools under the metal benches, train doors are closing, a low whistle.

later

Fluorescent headlights, an oversized jumper pressed against the mural, behind a cardboard sign, an outstretched arm. Light pools on the floor of the underground tunnel, reflecting against the walls. A long concrete spine intersecting the platforms. He waits on a station bench to Rookwood. On the floor, a teenage girl under a blanket, her back to the wall. He can see the outline of her knees, pulled to her chest, a small dog beside her.

Three days since he left—they've probably called his case worker. Or the police. He's not going back, he needs something to eat.

Trains arrive, the crowd disembarks, swelling at the escalator, flowing through the turnstiles.

He's tightening the straps of his backpack, slipping past them, towards the stairs. There are more sleeping bags, close to the underpass, a discarded trolley piled with plastic bottles, a face, momentarily covered as he passes.

He's at the bottom of the stairs, on the platform, folding his change into his pocket, where he'd stood with Evelyn and Mitch.

Hands please, hold the rail.

Platform 18. Still.

Behind the yellow line boys.

When he's settled, he'll call Evelyn. When he's got a plan.

Doors, stairs, seated, patterned swirls, red, wrinkled against his back. Resting his feet on the low metal bar, heels against the seat in front. ~~Central.~~ *She loved you so much, more than anything.*

Tunnels, cables, graffiti collages, electrical wires, then terraced roofs, back lanes and take-aways, dust and smoke, cars with open bonnets or missing parts, the smell of petrol, paint. *Let him answer for himself. Luke?* A strider, a cry, cables overhead. High-density apartments that seem to push against the elbow of the tracks as they bend and stretch towards Strathfield.

We have to say a proper goodbye today. All of us.

The flags are still there, on the roof of the old hotel, across the road from Lidcombe station. More of them, different ones. The post office has expanded, the chicken shop is boarded up, there's two newsagents now, one on each side of the street.
   Don't run. Take Mitch's hand.

Shutters, barely green, though the balcony looks freshly painted. Glass, fractured, yet suspended, frozen circular spirals in a low window behind the alley of the hotel. A yellow cone beside.
   Gates. Lidcombe entrance. Past another station, this one inside, now locked, vaulted, the Mortuary line.

Tree, path, open grass, shrubs, sticks, petals, ribbons, crosses.
   Come, I'll carry you. Please Luke. The Minister will be there already.

crooked   slanting   baked   marble   stone

Round the path, to the open field, the unmarked, to find that tree, that the nun had rested against, with the sunlight reflecting on the white calico shroud.
   Where he had stood, a hand on his shoulder. *God is looking after her.*
   His mum, discarded, beneath an unmarked tree.
   The Minister rushing his words, glancing at his watch, trying to catch the nun's eye. *May the Church be a comforting witness to Christ, to us all.*
   The tree had grown, but it was different. The shape of the trunk, the colour of the foliage. Sitting, to catch his breath, his heels against the soiled earth.
   For the grieving, for the sick, the dying, for those who rest with the Lord.
   It had lost its original shape, the tree was slanting.

For a mother, for a son. For those who cared for her in her illness. Comfort one another in this time of grief.

He remembered the nun would not look up.

He's running his hands over it. The bark had a different texture. It was brittle, flaked, he didn't remember the reddish colour inside.

May she be judged in mercy.

Around him, pebbles, weeds. The grass had come up to his knees.

The Minister had bent down to shake his hand, before turning, the grass dissolving under the hem of his robes. The nun had stayed behind, offering them tissues and sticky sweets from the hidden pocket inside her habit. He had chewed it while he made a bed of pebbles and flowers to place on top.

There was no grass, little crosses made from sticks, small stones and petals everywhere. All unmarked, beside leaves and shrubs and weeds and paths and stone and soil and foliage and rubble.

He pauses to watch a woman ahead of him on the path, she stops to lean down, laying flowers on the damp soil, beside another tree, like any other.

Evelyn had carried him back to the station, awake, he had kept his eyes closed, counting flowers and all the pebbles he had gathered, and the moment they had closed the box.

On the way back from the cemetery, he falls asleep.

The train loops past Town Hall, and Central.

Outside, the sharpened edge of a cruise ship, smudged blue against flaked clumps, scattered in the sky above the bridge.

Two-steps at a time, out of the station, before the doors catch his backpack.

He's along the walkway, beside the froth and the jetties, toward the forecourt on the eastern side.

With Evelyn, they had turned left, with a bag on each of her shoulders, pausing by the rails to offer them sandwiches or bits of crackers in foil. He leans over, squeezing his sandals between the metal rods.

The foam is reaching up to his toes. Evelyn is shaking her head. *Save the ice-cream till afterwards*. Mitch is rolling his eyes, reaching for a gummy snake, or a pink and green candy wrapper, from the pocket of his shorts.

She turns away to zip up their bags.

His feet are hurting but it's getting late and they can't walk it in the heat of the day. In front of them, a crowd, a short man covered in blue paint, his yellow hands pointing towards clouds. Mitch is copying his gestures. *He'll see you. Looking away. Mum, does it come off? Would he make the pavement blue?*

I don't know. I don't think he's supposed to sit down. Come on boys, please. I don't have any small change.

Past crowds, a cottage, up the hill beside concrete and water, to the foot of the bridge, through curved steps, covered, until they reached the top and Evelyn has to stop again, despite the elbows pushing past them, to find their caps and some sunscreen.

There's an army boat, a ship, part camouflaged against the glare, in the distance. He's not tall enough, but he can still make out the shape through the rims. Paper boats, rocks, the fins of the Opera House, a ferry (not a steamer) across the bay. Beside him, the long metallic tongue of the bridge. Shouldered behind: two domed towers and a ferris wheel, a spinning coin of blue, green and red, beside the face at the entrance of Luna Park.

Lunch before ice-cream, please don't ask me again.

There are plaques, unfamiliar, lighter grey than the stoned tiles embedded on the walkway. Evelyn had turned left out of the station, towards the bridge. A maze of metallic graves, circular, leading him towards the steps of the forecourt.

With the straps of his backpack tightened, Luke walks. Past buildings edged beside the Botanical Gardens, their long shadows nudging the branches. Past sails, to the far end of the walkway, into the Gardens, blanketed and domed by the pendulous branches of the Port Jackson trees. Their underside—burnished, rust. The figs are out, some without stalks, protruding, in pairs, waiting, drooping, beneath the dark canopy.

Beside singlets and tracksuits and the intermittent gurgle or cough from inside the prams, parked beside him, draped with muslin netting or a waffle blanket, to filter out the afternoon sun. Then on fold-up mats, flicking away pebbles and soil, beside the wheels of the pram, or on benches, arms motioning forward, then back. He can't call Evelyn, not yet. The shadows between the trees are stretching, reaching towards night. Bottles are being unlatched, lidded, tucked in a pouch beneath the bassinet or behind the seat, to be sterilised at home, after dinner.

Luke sits alone, on the brick rim of the path. The park ranger seems young, not that much older than him. His gaze is fixed on the water. He's got a slight lisp. Gates close at 6 p.m. He hides in the rose garden while the guard does his final round.

There's a pain below his left ankle. He sits up on the bench. The gardens are dark, the moon is a small splinter. He lies down on the bench again and falls asleep. Aerial roots and branches fold around him, squeezing him. He's reaching for a fig, its milky sap melting into his palms. The outside staining his fingertips copper, the underside of the leaves expanding inside his top, then bracing his wrists beneath its limbs. He sits up suddenly, calling out, grazing his knee on a low rock beside the bench, watching the fence that spans the perimeter of the Gardens.

His mouth is so dry he can barely speak. Heels beneath his backpack, but there is nothing to cover his chest, shoulders.

He needs to find a tap. He'd passed a sign, yesterday, to the toilets, close to where the prams were parked, but they'd be locked still, without a doubt, until the gates re-open at eight. He's scraping his tongue against the back of his palette, there's a rattling from inside his jaw.

Two hours, maybe more, till light. The carer would have called the police by now, or at least his caseworker.

This time it's not in his dream. The Gardens are dusted in flakes of sunlight. He can hear wheels, skidding on the concrete pavement. Prams are pouring in. Arms, chunky fingers making patterns in the air, a dropped teething ring and a wail. Luke is blinking his eyes, reaching for his backpack. He's got to move before the guards spot him. His ankle is swollen.

The leaves are still velvet, rust, luminous, from the water, reflected —the outline of a ferry.

In the afternoon, he wanders down, past the Botanical Gardens, along the peninsula, stopping beside the exposed sandstone rock, carved into a bench, overlooking the harbour, with an inscription, engraved like a headstone into the rock, built by convicts in the early 1800s, for the wife of the governor, a vantage point, to admire the incoming ships.

It's getting dark, he heads back along the path, to find somewhere else to spend the night.

His backpack is beneath the trees, across the lawn from the CBD, long fingertips of concrete and cladding, stretched against the evening sky.

It's after eleven.

He can't sleep.

He's lifting the cover off his sleeping bag, laying it flat between the fallen branches, ground pebbles and soil, then on his side, knees to his chest, hands beneath the flap of his jumper.

In the distance: sirens, the serpentine paths to the shoreline.

He's alone, in his old classroom, in his chair beside Sammy. Mrs B has gone to fetch a new duster for the chalkboard. His tummy hurts. Sammy is playing with a ball of hard gum, from beneath his chair. He leans over to the window, the tips of the leaves are edging through the gap in the window. The classroom door opens, it's the principal.

Mrs B will be back tomorrow. They have a new teacher, just for today.

He watches her enter, hair shiny, smiling, she sits down on the edge of his desk, watching him, then she wraps her arms around his shoulders, he can feel their eyes on her, she is holding his cheeks, asking him why he doesn't remember her. He does—but he can't place her. She has his mother's eyes and her cheekbones, but it's not her. At least he doesn't think so.

She is much older.

Now she's holding his hand, he won't look at her. The bell rings, he runs out of class.

When he looks back, she is still there.

The folds of her skirt reflected.

Luminous, in the glass panes.

He buys a roll for breakfast from the food court beside Circular Quay.

Watching the woman behind the counter as she puts on gloves to make the fillings and spread the sandwiches before the commuters, while he sits, picking at crumbs on the paper wrapping, elbows against the edge of the counter, on a plastic bar stool bolted to the tiles.

After breakfast he walks up the hill back towards the harbour, stopping to look behind him. He stops beside an old building, he looks up—there's a copper dome, a slate roof, balconies, parapets, a marble statue of Queen Victoria and the words 'PUBLIC ENTRANCE' carved beside him, in the sandstone, the old Chief Secretary's building, ornate detailing, constructed in stages.

There are no rangers, but there's nowhere to sit. On the benches, there are prams, parked, voices speaking softly into headphones. Further on, briefcases, backpacks and an early morning aerobics class.

He begins to recognise their faces.

During the days, seated, at the foot of the escalator to the train station, against the railings, beneath awnings and entrance steps, or on the low stone wall behind the gardens, as he makes his way to the public toilets.

But at night, they vanish, into the city's pockets. Seeking shelter within her curved bridges and archways or behind the pleats and the creases of ivy and weeds that grow over long-abandoned overpasses and walkways.

He'll try the Domain tonight. It's nearly sunset, the grass is empty. He's alone, beneath the trees, where once, in the midst of the Great

Depression, rows of homeless men, women, children, many of them soldiers, camped in the sprawling, shaded encampments.

The roots protrude through Luke's sleeping bag, he can feel them against his spine.

Tonight, instead of the edge of the Domain, where he is quilted beneath leaves, he unzips his backpack and lies down on the small patch of grass beside the fountains. He's looking upwards, the stars like yellow balloons, fading, as he turns onto his side.

This time, his mum looks younger, her cheeks are less drawn.

It's been raining, she's making him laugh, as they chase puddles, but his socks are wet, he starts to cry, takes off his shoes, he'll catch up to her, he's barefoot now, but she's too far ahead.

The pain is sharp, but it feels faraway, part of his dream, at first, until the weight on his chest propels him upwards, but there are only shapes, or a shape, clasping his wrists, his face, emptying the backpack that was beneath his head. Echoes, shouts, colliding on the grass, then they're gone, towards the trees, and the muffled city lights.

He should call Evelyn, but he can't like this.

The restroom cubicles are empty, his cheek is fluorescent, purple, he can't open his right eye properly. But they'll report him. Send him straight back. He'll ask for some ice at the food court.

Sitting, he'll attract more attention, so he follows the shoreline, loops back up the hill, then down towards the sails.

The months are passing, he's getting by.

Late afternoon, along the path to the water. The ferries are empty and shadows coat the underside of the branches, running, past the rose garden towards the stone gates, before sunset.

Outside, on the rim of the pavement, the motion of the tunnel, the soft lament and sigh of distant cars beneath his feet. Watching late night shoppers pool at the mouth of darkening buildings and emptying parking lots, to exhale crowds and commuters until the stations reopen for the morning.

Leaving him to roam, with an empty backpack, below the shapeless wings that hang from power cables beside the trees, behind the wall, closed, on the darkened city street.

One night, he notices a glow, illuminating, like a faint sketch, in yellow pencil, against the hard outline of the building ahead. It carries him, across traffic lights that don't change for pedestrians at this time of night, past pillars and marble, bins and plaques until he collapses beside the frame of a food truck, and a group of curious onlookers, perched, in lighted circles, on a collection of milk crates, camp chairs and tents.

It's the first proper food he's had in days, and a small tent, his own, well the camp's, but his for now, and blankets, socks.

When he's warm, there are questions. Lots of them, like him, running away from something or other, but he's welcome to stay, just watch himself and don't go bringing in anything stupid.

She leans back in her camp chair, watching him. He can call her Rae. Thirty years, give or take, not all the time of course. But better than that filthy accommodation they put you in, in between, didn't know a soul, took me three buses and over an hour to get back to the city to get my medication, if they show up, just refuse, tell them you'd rather be out here, I could've died in that place and they wouldn't have known for months, course they don't like us here, but we behave ourselves, but still, they don't like it.

The food truck is still there when he wakes up and unzips his tent, and there's a makeshift, fully stocked kitchen beside the laneway.

Cutlery, sauces, utensils, a gas-cooker staffed by a young woman, dishing corn flakes, or Weetbix in front of a large chalkboard with lines in white squiggles.

He's surprised to see that at the top of the next row, they've written his name.

I like to know who's who, says Rae, standing behind him with her plastic bowl raised for the milk.

The days fall into halves.

In the mornings, he joins the long line at the breakfast table, trying not to spill as he sits cross-legged with the mesh of his tent open, then to the amenities nearby, returning to pull out the plastic poles and fold up the cloth and frame, tucking them with his borrowed sweater, pants and toothbrush behind piles of camp chairs, folded and stacked against the wall behind the library. Then he walks, back towards the paths that sway and fold, like an untidy hem against the outline of the shore.

In the afternoons, the camp chairs are unfolded, no longer empty, laid out in rows that expand into uneven circular groupings.

He prefers to sit alone, close to the large fig tree that shades the camp, leaning his chair against the ridges of light grey bark, in the same position, furthest from the road, but even with his chair turned, there's a hand on his shoulder. The food truck lady's name is Emily, she's been volunteering for four years. Her husband too, on Thursdays the local restaurants chip in, and there's a bag of spare clothes in the truck. He can take whatever he needs.

He doesn't answer, but it's the same every afternoon after the food crates are unloaded, until he finds himself at the back of the truck, with Emily and her husband, holding a beanie, gloves, an extra blanket and a fleece hoodie. Trust me, you're going to need it. They've donated pizza. He eats beside Emily, the boxes stacked against the table.

They do come, in weekly rotations, photographing everything, even the folded camp chairs, bleached in the afternoon light.

The social worker's glasses are streaked with bands of brown and yellow, her auburn hair looks almost gold in the light. There are alternatives, you know.

She could be one of his teachers. She is squinting, kneeling, gesturing towards him. He shakes his head, concentrating on the plastic poles which are crossing out of sequence, causing the roof to bend, turning away until she moves on, to the tent behind, and that night, instead of watching the distant lighted towers, he sits, not on the grass or near the wall, but beside them, near the kitchen, in their circle, on their pavement, illuminated by the truck's headlights, then torches, and a portable heater.

    A few months after his arrival,
        instead of following the paths towards the sails,
        Luke finds himself beside flagpoles,
        lamp-posts,
        fluted marble columns,
        then at the top of the steps,
        outside to the library,
        he pauses to survey the bronze shapes,
        a woman holding a baby,
        a man beside water, groups of them, together,
        inside the patterned frames of one set of Portico doors,
        on the other doors, sails, masts, hulls, wigs, buttons, collars,
        and braids,
        behind him, in the distance, two cranes,
        on opposing sides of a scaffolded tower,
        their neck almost adjoining, a temporary spire over cladding.

Without warning, the bronze doors open and Luke enters the library, to be ushered straight out again, back down the steps, by an elderly man in uniform.

But instead of moving on, he sits on the bottom step, his back to the marble columns grouped in pairs, their hollow grooves like vertical tracks in stone. At lunchtime, the guard walks down the stairs, holding a paper bag, crossing the road that leads towards the gardens.

Then Luke is up the stairs again, his hand against the outline of shapes, pushing against the weight of the library doors.

Beneath him in the library foyer—vestibule, a map spiralled in marble, a replica, hand-drawn, ships and coastline inside a large mosaic, to his right, a wide staircase.

Ahead of him—the main library—rows of desks, rectangular, like wooden caskets beneath the sunlit panels, hugged by stained glass windows and the vertices of a large octagonal clock, he sits, alone on a long low bench opposite the eastern wall, on grey cushion encased in a rectangular wooden frame, reading the words carved in stone, reflecting the light.

A young guard is watching him from the door, behind a glass panel. She makes no sound and turns away to check the contents of a patron's bag.

His sobs are getting louder, an elderly woman with a shoulder bag pauses before the locker room to stare at him, the guard meets his eye, she's gesturing to a box of tissues on the desk.

He should leave but doesn't. He can't stop staring at the carved letters, he should remember her, but there's nothing, no grave, no headstone, no flowers to lay, no one to make him do his homework or take a shower, he can't even remember her smile.

The library doors are heavier from the inside.

Once he's down the stairs, he heads back to the camp, to put up his tent.

Emily comes looking for him, later on, when he doesn't join the dinner queue with the others. Rae saw him crying, she can take a break from cleaning up, if he wants to chat. But Luke shakes his head. She doesn't leave, she reaches down, picking up the small picture frame beside his backpack, studying it, barely blinking.

She was beautiful Luke, you look so much like her. I'm sure she adored you.

He's pulling a blanket over his head, closing the mesh, Emily is still watching him, he can hear Rae's voice outside the tent, he doesn't know why they even care.

He's awakened, around midnight, by a new arrival. Rae is shaking her head at the boy, but she lets him sit down and unpack his sleeping bag and she gestures to the spot by the wall where the tents are packed away. But the boy doesn't move, just lies down, on the paving, where he sat, and closes his eyes.

He'll sort the tent out tomorrow.

She stands near him for a few minutes, watching him, motionless, horizontal, a shadow on cold concrete, her eyes narrowed.

His name's Nate, they only let him out a couple of days ago, he's got nowhere to go, but they let him out anyway, told them he'd go back to the last home and it was all arranged, except he gave them the slip at Central Station where they were supposed to pick him up, he's done them a favour really, they're a bit sick of him and the feeling's mutual. His arm is knocking against Luke's elbow as they wait in line. Starving, I mean they feed you alright but … you don't want to have to spend too long in those cubicles.

It's nice to meet you too, Nate.

Emily is lowering her voice, watching them both, she pauses, pulling Luke to one side. Look, Rae mentioned they're expecting another visit, today or tomorrow, her eyes are on Nate, it's hard to know what time exactly, they come when they like.

At lunchtime, they're sitting, cross-legged, on the edge of the highway, Nate is barefoot, smoking, they taught me nothing, nothing much anyway, I never smoked before.

Luke is sitting with Emily behind the kitchen, It's not yet six, the tents are still closed, he's barely slept.

I'm not saying he's trouble, but he's *troubled*, it's his fourth, maybe fifth time with us. Rae is worried, just be careful. He comes and goes, but it always ends the same way. You're a good kid, you've just been through a lot of crap, but Nate, he's different, we've tried, every time he comes, we try, but he's … he's not open to changing. Now come on, help me set up, before the stampede.

It's after lunch and already Rae is having words with Nate. (In your tent!) The council will have a field day when they arrive. Not just three of them, like last time, but at least eight, grouped together. Luke recognises the lady who steps forward. We've had multiple complaints, unfortunately, businesses and some residents. Noise mostly, but other issues too. The bags, for example, the chairs, you can't leave them next to the wall like that, it's a trip hazard. Staff can't access the fire escape. And one of the residents has been smelling smoke, I'll need to inspect, please ask them to step outside.

Nate steps forward, his hand nearly touching her face, she steps back, an older man moves forward in her place.

I've got nothing to hide you motherfuckers!

He stumbles forward again, towards them, but Rae blocks his way.

Get out of here Nate, they're just doing their job.

Before she can stop him, he has bent down, his arms are closing around the rim of the camp chair that she had been sitting in, then lifting it, as if in slow motion, propelling the chair towards the council inspectors, watching it fly over their heads, landing upside down, in the road behind them.

The older man, closest to the street, waits until the cars have skirted around the chair, and then steps into the middle of the intersection to retrieve it. Placing the chair on the ground beside Nate, he summons his staff in low whispers and with a final glance, they are off. Rae follows, stepping into the road, calling after them, shrilly, but they have already crossed, in the direction of the station.

Luke finds Nate on a bench near the water, his eyes redder than usual, his knees pulled towards his face. He sits down beside him. Rae sent this, he's unwrapping one of Emily's cheese rolls. Nate stares at the plastic cling wrap but doesn't move, Luke shifts closer. It was a bit dumb, I guess, but they don't know, they don't give a shit about me, do they? Rae means well. Nate's wiping his nose on his sleeve.

Across the harbour, a ferry is docking, passengers are disembarking, others lined up to take their place, but on their side, the water is quiet, stagnant almost, Luke takes off his shoes, placing them beside his, beneath the bench. Nate is smiling again, reaching into his jacket pocket for a lighter, calling out to a group of girls, who ignore him, walking on. In front of them, a mother has paused to peg the edges of a muslin wrap over the front of her pram. She glances back at the smoke rising from the bench, turning away from them with an exaggerated cough, palms on the foam handles, walking, then running, along a path of late afternoon sun.

Nate is pulling his arm, his eyes fixed on the water. Now he's lacing up his trainers, trying to keep up, through the Gardens, towards the waiting ferry.

He's never jumped a turnstile before, he's too breathy to speak.

Nate is resting his feet on the empty plastic chair beside them, at the end of the pier.

The terminal is almost deserted, the ferry door opens as soon as they sit down, there's a small gap, between the gangway and the water, no one asks to see a ticket, they sit inside, beside a rectangular window, a porthole, the chairs are spongy, green, patterned with webbed branches.

The ferry pulls away slowly, then out into the harbour. Nate wants to go outside, the door is glass, heavy, they move to the side deck, sitting on a row of empty benches, beside a pole, knotted with thick rope around it.

The water is calm, behind the boat, a trail, milky, froth.

They disembark at the edge of the peninsula, in a small bay, beside a fish and chips shop, tea gardens, a playground.

The beach is beside the small pier, where the ferry is still docked. To their right, rows of small boats, empty, moored. Across from them, the city, spread out, glistening, silver, long rectangular charms, reflected on the surface of the bay.

Nate is already in the water, his t-shirt and shoes in the sand.

Luke can't swim, he sits at the shoreline, the beach is thin, narrow, sloped, in high tide the waves spill onto the grassy path beside the sand.

The water is icy, the ferry is pulling away, Nate is swimming towards it, calling to him.

He's shaking his head, the tide has pulled back.

Luke sits on the wet sand, the afternoon clouds are orange, pink, hazy, swept in from the back-burning, on the outskirts of the city. The water is shallow, translucent, schools of small fish swim beside Nate.

Suddenly Luke's on his back, there's water, above his head, a wave, pushing, submerging him, hissing in his ears, pulling his hair, pouring out his nostrils, stinging, then it's gone, withdrawing, past his toes, still clumped in wet sand. He can hear Nate's voice, laughing, pulling him up, damp material against his face, seagulls, clouds, his nose running, drying his eyes on the edge of Nate's sleeve.

They stay till the last ferry, collecting shells in a small plastic container they find in the sand, their clothes almost dry from the afternoon sun.

It's already dark when the last ferry docks, headlights blinding them, no turnstiles to jump, they run across the pier, across the gangway, through the open doors of the ferry.

They disembark at Circular Quay, walking slowly along the dark, wide streets, towards the camp.

The lamps are on, the chairs still folded, piled up, where they were, by the wall, beside the fire escape, despite the council's orders.

The others have eaten, but Emily has leftovers in the truck, she brings them some towels first, they peg their damp shorts behind the camp chairs, dinner bowls balancing on their laps. Most of the tents are closed, zipped for the night, Rae is nowhere to been seen.

The following afternoon, she's back, in her usual chair in the middle of the camp, holding the remains of an envelope, re-reading the letter in her hand, her head pressed against her left shoulder, asking Emily to gather them over here please. They won't leave, of course.

They won't be made invisible and, where the hell would they go?

There are people she knows, lawyers, mostly, who do this sort of thing for free. She'll go, tomorrow even, they must, they have rights.

And the council has no proof, and the rest, a distraction really, easily fixable, and yet any excuse, to break them down, to take their camp, any reason and they'll leap at it. She's rising from her chair as she speaks, drawing a crowd beyond the camp, leather briefcases are placed on the ground, momentarily, in the sprint between meetings and social lunches, young executives pausing to watch the spectacle of an old homeless woman shouting, spirited, with a splintered stick, half-leaning on a camp chair.

Within a few weeks, there are truncheons patrolling the perimeter of the camp, along with the leather suitcases, who come to watch Rae's lunchtime rants.

Emily helps them to make signs, with the cardboard from the empty food boxes and when his arms get tired, Luke tapes his to the front of his tent.

Emily has the best handwriting, so after breakfast, there is another queue as the camp residents line up, holding out their cut-out cardboard and giving instructions across the makeshift table. Emily nods and scribbles accordingly, in bold font, in thick black texta.

No profanities, no threats, Rae's orders.

>   Save Our Camp   Peace   Feed Not Greed
>   The city is HOME to everyone
>   Don't Send US Away   Drug and Alcohol Free Safe Space
>   SAFE ON THE STREETS
>   Empathy, Compassion, LOVE
>   COMMUNITIES COME IN ALL SHAPES—JOIN US FOR A CUPPA
>   Don't let the Council
>   bury us—we are still alive!

But soon tourists, locals, are skirting around the camp, taking longer routes to avoid her shouts, the placards, the offices, just round the corner, have hired extra security guards, much to Rae's amusement, buffoons, but they're there, hovering nearby enough that, instead of arranging the camp chairs in overlapping circles after dinner, to chat loudly beside the radio in the makeshift kitchen, the residents, even Rae, speak in low voices and head early to zip up their tents. They won't even look at us any more.

Luke can see Emily watching them from inside the food truck. He turns away, heading back towards their tents.

Just drop it Nate, please.

At lunchtime the following day, Nate and Luke follow Rae, along with Emily and about two dozen residents, their signs, raised high, walking, as if in slow motion along the perimeter of a wrought iron fence, vertical bars, elongated, beneath rows of sharpened pickets, in the shadow of a long, low building.

Maroon columns are framed by several hanging lamps, glass, ornately carved, suspended from the ceiling about the doorway beside the façade, rum hospital, surgeon's quarters, renovated, restored, twinned, through a roof garden and fountain court, with a concrete slab, offices, that sit, sombre, hunched and partially hidden, behind the stately Victorian exterior.

Her high-pitched voice has already attracted attention; the security guard has stopped scanning handbags and is walking down a wide staircase towards their group.

She's deflated, she won't look up. Emily brings a plate, plastic utensils, even a tray, so she can have dinner in her camp chair, but she shakes her head, shoos her away, she's got to plan, she can eat in the morning.

No one's ever seen her like this.

I've known Rae, on and off, twenty years, she fell down an escalator at the train station, about twelve years, ago, and she was hobbling around in plaster, but she was still coming to find us in the Gardens, her hat had even more coins than usual, she said we could all buy something together.

You know, she was married, a long time ago now, he used to beat the shit out of her. She told me she got up one morning, put her passport in her handbag, left her front door keys in the post box and got on a bus.

It's after 1 a.m., maybe 2, Luke can't bring himself to open his eyes, he's lying on his side, but he's not asleep, his pupils can't focus properly.

What's the point even?

She hasn't come to him, not for a while now, a few weeks at least, even though she's always different, in small ways, even though he's never sure, in the moment, or when he wakes up, if it's really her, he misses the feeling, the hoping, that maybe it was.

Hands are unzipping his tent, it's Nate. He needs to come inside, now, someone had to, but maybe now, he should leave, before Rae wakes up.

His eyes can't focus, he feels half asleep, but he hasn't slept.

Nate is dragging his arms, lifting his legs.

Please just have a look, I don't know. I had to do *something*.

Luke is standing now, bending over, as he steps out of the tent.

Against the chalky light he can make out words, over-sized, patterns and swirls, a multi-coloured web of graffiti, on the sandstone wall in front of him, beside the fire escape, where their folded camp chairs are piled, against council orders, in a sort of lop-sided pyramid, some with covers on, necks of string, closed firmly around them.

Luke recognises the photographer, and the council worker with the short hair. But they're accompanied, this time, by two policemen, scribbling in notebooks, glancing in the direction of the wall.

I know you're angry Nate, about our situation, I am too. But it's a heritage-listed building for goodness sake.

He's got two, three days at the most, to make other plans. When she stops shouting, when she's cleared her throat, Rae passes him a piece of folded paper. It's only temporary accommodation, but it's something. Call them. I'm not a fan myself but for a young fellow like you, it will be fine. He is looking past her, at the last scraps of afternoon light, reflecting against the water. It's not personal, I hope you can see that, but I can't have you come back again.

The policeman is gesturing for her, it's unfortunate, they've been warned. They're just more than fifty of them now, they can't leave, not over this.

Nate won't come out of his tent, not even on his last night, to say goodbye to the others. Not even for pizza, that Emily got as a special favour, for him.

Luke helps him fold away his tent, bedding.

He's got to walk to the station early; the hostel is an hour away, more or less. They won't let me smoke there, will they?

He leans in closer, looking around.

Listen Luke, when they come back again, you can't screw it up, you're not chicken shit, you have to fight.

Rae's a lot happier, from the moment Nate heads off, backpack over his shoulders, in the direction of the station, plus she's going to see the lawyer today, there's always a long queue, but they'll find a way, if she gets there early.

She's back after five, jubilant. There were at least twenty ahead of her, but she waited, they saw her, by mid-afternoon, they listened, there are ways, lots of ways, she's not sure exactly how long.

When Luke comes back from the toilet, it's almost dark, Emily and her husband have decanted the cereal boxes from the breakfast tables into the back of the truck, and they're securing the legs of the two trestles, joining them together to form a long rectangle partitioned by plastic tablecloths, overlapping, hanging neatly, pressed against two dozen camp chairs, beneath a knotted rope of fairy lights.

They can't all fit, but there's a ring of extra chairs around the edges, a few feet back from the table, with small crates to balance the extra plates on.

Luke is helping to lay out the plastic plates and cutlery when Rae opens her tent to see the festivities and Emily ushers her to sit, at the centre of the table, her chair illuminated by a pink light from the arched windows behind, carved like a deep graze and knitted, into the edges of surrounding stone.

She has tears in her eyes.

Emily is laughing as she hands around the greasy cardboard boxes, still warm, they have reasons to celebrate, Luke sits beside her, in Nate's camp chair.

They've rotated now, so the others get a turn at the table, and a second serving appears from the truck. She is refilling the cordial, Rae is reaching for a pocketknife to slice her food. The tablecloths are awash in crumbs and turned over cups.

Do you think he'll go? To the accommodation? Even for a few nights. But Emily just shrugs, she can't hear him, someone has turned up the volume on the portable radio. Luke can't switch off, the hostel is miles away, he'll never see him again.

Rae is smiling but she sits with her head bowed, towards the pavement, eyes lowered, as if in disbelief, her pocketknife clean again, folded, neatly balanced, on the rim of the crate.

Around her, swinging arms, a hand on Luke's back, rotating chairs and music, barely audible over the voices, the faces, turned inwards, towards each other, deep in conversation, animated, oblivious to the traffic, the wheels, side bumpers that slow and seem to kiss the edges of the pavement, beside the food truck, as they pass.

Rae tells them about the stars, she knows all the names, the positions, even Emily is looking up, towards the charcoal sky, as she talks. They sit, silent, lulled by her voice, on camp chairs, crates, crossed legs on the concrete. Below the Southern Cross and Venus, hanging low in the night, luminous, like a clock, beginning to fall.

She goes around the jagged circle, asking, one by one, about their day, how they're feeling, if she can help in some way.

Then she turns up the radio, the camp chairs are emptied, there's clapping, dancing, beside the portable heater, the crates a ring of drums, beating, broken intermittently, by distant sirens.

It's after midnight when Luke helps them to drag the trestle tables back towards the makeshift kitchen. Emily insists on laying on out the breakfast things, in case someone gets hungry.

The batteries have been taken out of the radio, most of the tents are zipped now, but Luke is still out, bent down on the pavement, piling discarded crusts and dropped cups into a large plastic bag, Rae is sitting at the edge of her tent, watching him.

We're going to be ok, all of us. Luke pauses, nodding. The pink glow from the windows behind them has faded, but the stars are like a thousand torches, blinking without rest.

You've done plenty Luke, I'll see you in the morning.

He's slept two, maybe three hours, when there's a jolt, a hand fumbling with the zip of his tent, then Emily's voice, muffled, crying, screaming something that he can't understand.

His small alarm clock has run out of batteries, he's sitting up, trying to find his hoodie, Emily is pulling at his arm, begging him to stand up.

His back catches against the flap of material as he half stands, then bends, knocks his shoulder, staring into the light, beside voices shouting, sirens, shapes running in the dark, as policemen begin to throw their pile of folded camp chairs, beside the sandstone wall, without pause, into the back of the waiting trucks.

Rae has climbed onto a crate, she's waving her stick, below her, the ground is strewn with blankets, bedding. Move on, move on or get into the trucks as well. Luke trips over a crate as he heads towards her, there are stray bits of clothing, everywhere, on the ground.

The glare from the headlights burns against the darkness,
with their torches, police go from tent to tent,
ripping them open, as toiletries, jumpers,
shoes are thrown into bags or flung towards the waiting trucks,
to join the growing mass of pillows and blankets.

Shapes knock against him as he bends down on the ground to find his backpack. It takes three officers to lift the two-seater couch, despite the headlights and the stars, he can see almost nothing.

Some of his belongings are scattered
where his tent stood.

A voice that sounds like Emily's is screaming, but her cries are muffled by the sirens. Even the branches of fig tree seem lower, stooped, Luke can almost touch them.

    Near the makeshift kitchen, Emily's husband is standing between
    Rae and a police officer, her stick is on the ground beside her,
    snapped in two,
    she is leaning one hand on Emily's husband's shoulder,
    in the other—the open glimmer of a silver blade,
    Luke rushes towards the pocket knife,
    but before he can reach her, Rae is shoved off the crate,
    to the ground, her elbow bone cracking against the concrete,
    two officers standing on top of her, Luke is screaming,

Emily has found him, she saw it too,
her husband is trying to reason with the officers,
she's over seventy for Christ's sake,
you better call an ambulance, she's still hissing,
spitting towards them, swearing, if Nate was here,
if,
Emily is crying, pleading for them to get off her.

She is battling to speak, her ribs are cracked, and still, items are being flung back and forth, tents being dismounted, bodies crouching, running, shouting, looping all around them, a small crowd gathering when word spreads that it's Rae, they haven't taken all the camp chairs, not yet.

Luke walks silently over to the wall, grabbing the first chair he can find, it's folded, knotted, the metal legs are the sharpest part, it's surprisingly heavy.

He's behind the policeman now, Rae's feet are motionless, she's quietening down, but she can't stop shaking her head, side to side, then again, side, side, side, the officer is still sitting on her, he can hear her wheezing, gasping for breath under the weight of his torso.

Then he's swinging the chair, the legs of the chair, towards the police officer, but he misses, again, the chair is too heavy, he can't help Rae, her screams are muffled by the pavement, then he can feel gravel, small pebbles scratching his face. He's on the concrete next to her, a second officer securing his arms behind his back.

Early morning. The stars seem to have fallen, the sky is empty, the wind has come up. Rows of figs hang, in the branches above the camp, like eyes, in pairs. The tree is sombre, upright, watching, its dark green leaves coated with damp tears, from the early morning dew.

Another four police cars arrive. More sirens. The trucks are filled up.

Rae's received a caution. She's on the way to hospital.

In the back of the food truck, her possessions are gone. Emily has a black eye. Her husband is on the phone to a lawyer.

Luke can't make out any more through the tinted windows of the police car. Metal cuffs binding his wrists. Driving away. To the station. Before he has a chance to fetch his backpack or say goodbye.

The hauling goes on for hours. The Council arrives by 5 a.m. The morning is clear. They've driven their vans onto the pavement. Beacons for oncoming traffic. Only fragments left now.

The odd crate. Several garbage bags. Unclaimed clothes. Lined up. In neat rows. Along the wall. Where the camp chairs were stored.

A worker in thick gloves is picking up stray cutlery.
    A few plastic bottles.
            Even a stray boot that has landed up in the bushes.

The makeshift kitchen like the residents and even the police are gone. But the large chalkboard which stood behind the breakfast table is still there. It's not that heavy. But it's been left behind. Rows and rows of names. Fifty of them. Fifty-one, if you include Nate. Etched in squiggly cursive. Not Emily's doing. Rae herself. Not her name though. But everybody else's. The council worker steps closer to inspect the chalky scribbles. Retreating to his van. Returning minutes later.

With an extension cord and a thick green garden hose.
                                        Its coils twisting and crooked
as water lashes from its serrated metallic tongue.

after

| | | | | | |

No food comes, Luke's knees to his chest,
sideways, against the floor, concrete, smooth,
except for small etchings, like mottled skin,
near the wall, tiny words, scribbled, just above
floor height, names he doesn't know.

He's hooked his arms inside his top, for warmth,
pins and needles below his right knee, he's got
no jumper or blanket, when I'm ready you piece
of shit, we'll see.

That was earlier, his eyes are closing, no sounds
from beneath the door and still, above him,
that luminous, flickering light, a pale rectangular tube,
watching him, with an irregular, hissing pulse.

In his dream, there's a low wall, the stones at one
end are uneven, they've been like that since before
he started school. It's near the bottom of the school sports field,
they would pass it every day, together,
on the way to school, but then take the shortcut
home. There's a crowd gathered out front, not
quite in a line, but they're waiting, graffiti, small bits
of paper, folded and tucked between the boulders.
Behind them, a door, wooden, panelled, carved into
the chest of the wall, and a small wooden chair out front.

His legs feel heavy, swollen, he talks to them, but
they won't answer, his chair rattles against the pavement
when he stands up. He's pacing, up and
again, beginning where the rocks are missing their top layer, and then
back, watching as the door opens, intermittently, after each name on
the list is called. He could push the door open, but he's not allowed to,
and he'd need help, plus he's supposed to be home already, it's almost
dinner time. But when he starts walking, he's barefoot, the chair is still
by the door, it's back straight, facing away from the wall, he sits again,
then crouches, beneath the chair, to see if his shoes are underneath.

He can't open his eyelids until he rolls over, his chin
pressed downwards, embracing the floor, a horizontal
slab, stiff, sallow, glassy against his palms.

From the corridor, whimpers, cries, breathless boots.

| | | | | | |

They don't greet him, when he hands in the form, on the other side of the metal detectors. The office is white, the shelves almost empty, he can see the guard's mouth, moving, behind the thick, dulled glass. Through the gap, a hand, sliding a small container.

He'd been sitting, for hours, in front of the glass panel, in the middle seat, in a row of five, plastic, melded together, bolted legs on either end, a small black handrail between each chair. Behind him, more rows, empty, beside the dark steel lockers, with their orange tongues and a small, bolted window.

Classes follow the school calendar, Monday to Friday, programs on the weekends, instructions, respect, to staff, other youth, hygiene, bedtime. Smokes, swearing, violence, graffiti, inappropriate touching, breaking anything (including the fire alarms/cameras/sprinklers/anything), you'll be visiting our Behavioural Management Section.

They send him to a room to change. He can barely open the door. There are stains on the leg of the pants, the underwear is too loose, he could tuck in the shirt, but the Velcro on his right shoe doesn't close properly. They can't have laces. Everything is washed, at least.

On the wall, un-laminated posters: no alcohol, drugs, excessive personal medication, mobile phones, devices, computers, memory sticks, explosives, wire, rope, tools, metal cutlery, aerosols, toy guns, umbrellas, magnets, wax, plasticine, chewing gum, Blu-Tack, newspapers or magazines.

Do you know about any young persons offering gifts to staff?

Cling film, tin foil, vinegar, and craft glue are permitted, in small quantities, but will be closely monitored.

Have you seen any staff or young people participating in corrupt behaviours?

When he's done, they unlock the door. His clothes, fleece jumper, the framed photo that he had rescued from his tent, his backpack, pillow, wallet, pre-paid mobile phone that Emily had arranged for him, are swallowed, sealed in the lockers.

In the plastic container: a comb, moisturiser, deodorant (roll-on), a miniature bottle of shampoo, toothbrush and paste, a reusable water bottle. It all fits, lid on, through the gap, except for the empty bottle, which is passed to him separately. The guard turns away, he's still gripping the container, watching, the circular motion of fingers on the keyboard, across the glass.

| | | | | | |

Fluorescent shadows, sixteen doors, split on each side of the corridor, glass panels cut, narrow, into the upper half of each door that waits: motionless, blinded, bolted. Beneath the long halogen tubes, facing forward, his eyes scanning the glass panels. At the foot of each door— a square hatch, just large enough to fit a small tray through.

Behind the panels, faces, turned away, bolted stools, one turning, meeting his eyes, rising from his stool to pound the door with the flat of his hands. The guard walks on, without turning his head, Luke follows, behind.

The bed is unmade, a blanket, sheet, pillow, towel, a small desk and stool, both fastened to the floor, no seat on the toilet, a low basin. Beside the basin, the remains of a bar of a soap. He can pace the length of the cell in four steps. The door is latched behind him. He sits on the edge of the bed, unfastens his Velcro shoes, stands up again, barefoot, leaning over the desk. On a small shelf above the desk, he arranges them, in descending order: the water bottle (re-filled from the basin), closest to the wall, then moisturiser, deodorant, the small shampoo, toothpaste, the toothbrush and the comb, horizontal, jagged, in the row in front.

He had tried to wave, Emily couldn't see him, it was still dark, when she had banged on the back of the police van, her hands streaking the thick glass window, trying to see inside. Reaching for a crate or a box in the rubble (anything not yet piled onto the trucks), when it reverses, over the pavement, still quilted in damp leaves and small branches (pulled apart by birds, cockatoos, trying to reach the figs) and sending Luke sliding towards the other plastic bench, in the back of the van.

He can only shower in the mornings, the blanket is thin, yellowed, but under the light (a long, fluorescent tube, like the passageway), his desk is stone, white, the bed, tinged green.

The lights inside their cells go out soon after dinner. But the tube from the passageway stays on, stretching down beneath his door, edging shadows, by the foot of his bed. If he puts the blanket over his head, they'll bang on his door, three times and then open it, shining a flashlight in his eyes, to write him up for a disciplinary violation. From the corridor, voices, slammed doors, a vacuum cleaner.

| | | | | | |

He can hear noises though the wall of his cell, his eyes close eventually—he's in a home he doesn't recognise, he can't find his sleep toy, he promised Mrs B he would look after it, the foster carer unpacked the plastic bags, he's running to her room, crying at the door, she's in her dressing gown, he needs to calm down, she hasn't seen the toy, she's absolutely positive, it wasn't in the plastic bags. He's sitting against the wall, in the pyjamas she lent him, he can't sleep without Little Cat, he's banging his head against the wall, again and again, he's got to stop that or he'll hurt himself, her husband is yelling from the bedroom, she'll find a different sleep toy for him in the morning, he's got to go back to bed.

| | | | | | |

He's been dozing, on and off, for a couple of hours, his face turned away, from the corridor, the night-light, the chatter, the doors, when there's a shriek, from the cell across from him, from a boy he hadn't spoken to, but had sat next to, in the dining hall, who is throwing things now, his deodorant can, water bottle, comb, even the small shampoo, at the metal bars, spitting, at the guards behind. Confiscated, all of it, except the water bottle, but soon he starts pounding at the bars with disfigured plastic, then that, too, in the bin and the boy himself, cuffed, face down on the ground, lifted by a pair of guards, for a late-night visit, to the Behavioural Management Section.

The night light has almost reached his toes, he's on the floor, learning against the bed, reflected against his desk, the outline of his uniform over the bolted stool, shadowed along the wall, he can barely swallow, his arms are holding his knees, rocking back, forth, there's a weight against his ribs, his chest is burning, but he's so hungry, he crouches down further, he can taste acid, his knees, the floor, compressed against him. Moving backwards, away from the fingers of light, stretched out, bending towards him, from the corridor. His eyes are closing.

A guard is studying the logbook, in it, the day's incidents, recorded, surveyed, beneath the fluorescent tube, by night staff, pacing intermittently, to peer at them, through the glass. Across the passageway, another bang, raised voices, *stop looking for attention*, now seated once more, until the next rounds.

He can smell sandwiches, chicken, tuna mayonnaise from the canteen, but he has to stay, all of lunch, until the end-of-recess bell goes, the field outside is filled with moving shapes, small figures, like plastic, the field a damp board with curled up edges, from where he's standing, beside rows of empty chairs, at the classroom window.

A spasm in his neck, he's still on the floor, across from him, the shoes they gave him, he's awake, lifting the shoes towards him, pulling, at the Velcro, to open, close, open, open, open the straps, picking at the fluff, the hair, bits of dirt, stuck to the inside.

| | | | | | |

Morning, rows of tables, chairs, screwed to the floor, a bowl of corn flakes, a small carton of orange juice, before that, dressed, showered, it's not that bad, you get used to it, not the food though, never.

Doesn't bother me, it's my seventh time. I was fourteen the first one.

Turning to Luke, pushing against his shoulder. When you fight, you've only got a few seconds, they break it up pretty quick, you have to work on your technique, you have to do it quickly.

He can feel eyes burning the back of his head. A guard that wasn't there last night, a barbed wire ring tattooed on his upper arm. Moving closer.

Behind him, other boys.

I can show you, if you need.
It's so boring, they're worse than the teachers where I went.
They're fucking psychos.
I'm hungry, you know, at night mostly.
Shut up.
Didn't they used to give us meat?
Hey, my girlfriend just got a new phone.
It's to save money you idiot.
Have you ever jacked a car?

The new guard, Clyde, hunching over the rectangular table, the boys have stopped talking, his shoes are thick-soled, boots, high, above his ankles, like the ones in the photo, in Madga's study, his calves are bent forwards, gun tucked beside his belt, the lines of his chest, muscles, shirt tucked, tightly, into his khaki green shorts. The Centre nurse walks past, Clyde turns away from them, he's smiling, teasing her about her wedge shoes, offering to bring another chair, his elbows still resting on the tabletop. She's walking away, the strap on her handbag is twisted, she's a few tables away, still adjusting it. He turns back to them, sitting, at the edge of the table. His head is shaved, mostly, but not at the very top. The boy beside Luke is rocking, just slightly, backwards and forwards, in his plastic chair. The guard leans in, his face almost touching the boy, his boot against the metal leg of the chair. Across his upper arm, a barbed wire ring and a figure eight, inked, stained, on the underside of his wrist. The boy's chair is still. Clyde looks up, facing Luke now, his hand is paused, motionless, holding a plastic spoon.

| | | | | | |

They can kick a ball, not for long, but it's his first time outside, for exercise, the sky like grey chalk, the group of them, seated in line, along the rectangular yard and a pile of cigarette butts.

The boy whose cell is across from him kicks first. The others were distracted, still seated. Then another boy, with a broken front tooth, standing up, *you don't start till I call it*.

But the ball keeps on moving, knocking the perimeter of the fence, sending red dust up their nostrils, this time he lurches without a pause, towards the ball and the younger boy, his fists against ribs and cheekbones, then standing over him, pressing his right shoe harder, into his stomach.

The line parts, Clyde steps forward, both boys still, frozen, blood dribbling from a nose, onto the pebbly concrete turf.

It's over, the boys start walking away, to head back inside, but Clyde stops them, he's laughing, he's not scolding them, he's got a chocolate bar, from the vending machine, that he's pulling out of the pocket of his khaki shorts, holding it up over the boys' heads.

So, you wusses like to fight?

A taller boy, one Luke hasn't seen steps forward, nodding.

Clyde is nodding, watching, at the front of the line as the taller boy steps forward, towards broken tooth, one punch to his left cheek, then he's bleeding too, from both nostrils, on the ground beside the other boy.

He bends down, picks up the soccer ball and walks back towards Clyde, a look of expectation, longing, Clyde unwraps the chocolate bar, as if to eat it himself, then pauses, shoves it between the tall boy's fingers, slapping him, on the side of his arm. Then taking the ball.

| | | | | | |

Morning, a different guard, accompanying them, to the Learning Centre, across the grounds, still within the fence. The path is overgrown, the grass dry, colourless, itching against his ankles, the ground is brown, red, flat. There's no shade, no trees, only a few stumps where trees once stood, towering above the fence, stumps barely taller than the long grass, cut, felled, still rooted beneath the pebbles and soil. From above, concentric rings encircled in the stumps, light rings from spring and early summer growth, dark rings from late summer and autumn growth, dry seasons, droughts, rainy seasons, scars, from bush fires, recent and decades old.

The sky is like wool, thick, greying, distant, from the hazard reduction burns.

Luke recognises where he is, close to the front gates, he had arrived in the dark, under the row of searchlights, long necked, rising, even above the top of the fence, straight-backed, standing to attention.

Below, Luke's eyes stinging, squinting, luminous under the glare.

Despite the overcast weather, the lights are off today, watching, desolate, over the perimeter, as the group passes.

There are stop signs, other warning signs too on the front gates, a car outside uses the driveway to reverse, quickly, before changing direction, the street is empty otherwise, he remembers the gates, the lights, but not the street outside. Above, more barbed wire, sharp-tongued mesh coils, pulling faces from above the fence.

He pauses, looking back, towards the main building, it's lower, flatter, than the court that they had taken him to, alone. The heavy concrete arms of the Bidura Children's Court, that stands, adjacent to rows of narrow terraces and wrought-iron facades, the sharp, unplastered elbows of the building, stained, surrounded by litter, empty garden beds. In front of the Court, verandas, shutters, a ballroom, slate roof, two tall chimneys protruding from each side of a stately, rectangular house, for many years, a depot, receiving, holding, long rows of beds, empty or filled, children, waiting for court, or care, or somewhere else, temporary, transferring, the first place they saw, after they were taken, and changed, into blue uniforms, stockings, in the handsome Victorian villa, with its padlocks, kerosene and rags for lice, early mornings, beatings on wet sheets and cold floors, a timber fence.

One light ring, one dark ring, one year of a tree's life.
The guard is shouting at him, hurry, keep up with the other boys.

It's like a cottage, of sorts, square, stone, homely, only with the razor wire along the perimeter of the roof.
Out front, embedded into a concrete slab, the words,
>COURAGE
>RESILIENCE.

| | | | | | |

He likes her, Ms Ali, she's different, but somehow familiar. The windows of the classroom are bolted, outside the Learning Centre, two guards, waiting, grey through glass, but still, there's sunlight, coating the tables and chairs (shaped not in rows, but in a large square, fastened to the ground). Map of the states and territories, on the wall, a calendar, and a whiteboard, empty, when the group enters the room.

She puts Luke towards the front, he's missed almost a year, in the short break she calls him aside, there's a lot to catch up, but she understands, it's about filling in the gaps now. She wants to learn their names, the new boys take turns, walking to the front of the class, standing in front of the whiteboard, it takes him a few minutes to decide which colour, finally he writes his name, in bold font, in blue marker, near the top of the board, she smiles, but the boy behind him is knocking his feet against the leg of the table, refusing to stand up, that's ok, you stay put, I can write it for you.

Another boy, opposite him, is crying. Ms Ali fetches the box of tissues from her desk. He won't look up, she leaves the box on his table, standing in front of the group, then returning to her desk after handing out a maths worksheet. The boy wipes his nose, then crouches, picking at the spongy filling, the plastic covering of his chair, the other boys watching him, laughing, as he pulls bits of foam from his fingernails. I'm not doing it. I told you. I can't do maths Miss.

Ok you come sit here with me, we'll go through it together.

Luke gets up to empty his sharpenings, the bin is close to where Ms Ali sits, when her back is turned, he pauses, surveying the desk, there's a baby, dark-haired, only a few months old, smiling at him, with Ms Ali's eyes, from behind the glass of a wooden frame.

I'm not a five-year-old. I don't need your help.

He turns to the window, to his friends, fuck jail and school! Ms Ali is talking to him, so quietly Luke can't make out the words, but the boy has turned his head, he's reaching inside his chair, scooping out handfuls of foam, then without warning, the plastic cover is off, the boys behind him are out of their seats too, tackling each other as they move towards the chair, the fragments of broken foam, sprinkled, thrown, until the guards outside the window, ignoring Ms Ali's pleas, enter, restrain them, face down, faces in the foam.

There's another lesson after, once the four boys, two in front, two behind, two guards tailing, have left, cuffed, screaming, Ms Ali shaking her head, the classroom hosed in the mid-morning light, silent, for now.

| | | | | | |

weekday | wake | shower | dress | clean cell |
meal | school | meal | school | meal | unit-time | sleep |
weekend | wake | shower | dress | meal | program |
meal | rest | meal | sleep | weekday

| | | | | | |

A few weeks later, when he enters the dining hall, Clyde is waiting for him. In the guard's hand, there's a letter, he can see his name, in Evelyn's tidy handwriting.

The door to the dining hall opens, it's the Director, Clyde steps away, the thumb on his right hand still inside his pocket. He's standing with the Director, answering him, quietly, they're surveilling the room, the boys have stopped talking, they're pretending to eat. They walk together, between the tables, Clyde a few steps in front of the Director, clearing the empty chairs from their path. They stop by the door to the courtyard, watching a group of boys, exercising, through the glass. Clyde is looking down, his eyes fixed on the ground. He's nodding, nodding, agreeing, shaking the Director's hand, before he steps outside to greet the boys.

Clyde walks back, past the tables, towards him, pausing, before the door to the toilets, folding the letter for him, from Evelyn, placing it in the back pocket of his khaki shorts, the corner still visible, bent, below the rim of his polyester shirt.

He can see the Director, walking across the grounds, in the direction of the main gate, below the search lights, their long necks sallow, hung forwards. The boys outside are still exercising,

A few minutes later, there's shouting, from the boys' toilets beside the dining hall, Clyde is standing outside the door, holding a large packet of toilet rolls, still sealed, except for a small hole, punctured in the plastic.

One of the night guards walks past, pausing, to chat, his shoe kicking the toilet paper, they're both laughing now, leaning against the door, his boot still perched on the wrapped toilet paper, beside the sign, behind them, muffled shouts from the cubicles.

The boy to his left is flicking peas off his fork. Luke tries to swallow. A female guard is pouring juice, handing out disposable cups, to a row of Velcro shoes, shuffling, impatient, in front of the serving table.

| | | | | | |

The afternoon lessons drag, two other guards have taken over the window roster, Ms Ali looks tired, but her voice is enthusiastic, he prefers English to maths, she reads them a short story, the boys closest to the window are pulling faces, intermittently, at the guards, but only when their heads are turned, towards the main gates.

He tries to concentrate on her voice, but the boys next to him are talking in loud whispers, who they want to beat up, who's going to smack him first, who's going to take the pen inside his shirt when we leave?

He should call Evelyn. When they go to the phone booths, on Saturday.

They're repeating some spelling words, aloud, when a notebook hits him, from behind, on the shoulder, he stands up, looks around, he knows they're laughing, but no one looks him in the eye.

The boy behind gets up to throw his sharpenings away, elbowing the boy in the front row on his way to the bin, the other boy is taller than him, he's standing over him, his is going to be in the dustbin too, his head first, Ms Ali had raised her voice, she's standing between them, he's never heard her talking this loudly, but she's not shouting, she's calm, firm, the taller one has sat down again, she's pointing to the window, the guards are waiting for her cue, she shakes her head, one guard turns back in the direction of the gate, the other is still watching them, through the window, she's giving them a final warning, she knows their stories, they think school's a waste of time, she's not there to give them more punishment, she's trying to help them, giving them a way to move forwards, but it's not easy, she needs their help, they need hers.

Except for a few sniggers, and some more sharpenings poured on the floor, they are unusually quiet, cooperative even, for the rest of the lesson. The bell rings at four, they're allowed to go, but only after the guards have lifted their shirts, checked their shoes, emptied their pockets.

What will he say?

One of the guards walks in front, the other a few steps behind them, as they cross the grounds, he can hear distant voices, cars. The boys in front of them, huddling.

They think they're going to change me, but I block those pieces of shit out of my mind, they're nothing to me, nothing. I've got another three months, then I'm done. When I first got here, I had no feelings, like someone took away everything.

Did you notice?

The floodlights in front of them have flicked on, their long necks hunched, illuminated, watching.

Ms Ali, her titties. They're huge man, since she had that baby. Huge.

| | | | | | |

After breakfast, before school, the tables are being cleared, an older boy and Luke are spraying disinfectant, on the surface, the side, the chairs. They'll earn extra points, enough for something from the vending machine. His cloth is soaked with milk, cereal crumbs, spilt juice. He's also swept the floor, but there are more crumbs. He needs to rinse it off, in the sink, before they wipe again. Before he can head to the kitchen, the door opens, Clyde is beside them, snorting, the cleaning cloth has fallen to the floor, Luke bends down to pick it up, the older boy hesitates, then angles his spray bottle, spraying disinfectant into the guard's face, for a moment Clyde stands motionless, staring, before picking up the broom, from the floor, beside Luke, and then imprinting it, in horizontal lines, across the front of the boy's legs.

He can't keep up with the lessons this morning; he can still see the lines on the boy's legs. What if Mitch answers the phone? Mid-morning, Ms Ali has a surprise. Someone has a birthday, today, she's got the kitchen to provide a small cake, the boys refuse to sing, but they're out of their chairs, lining up, it's already pre-sliced, he eats his in three bites, it's enough to get him through the morning, she calls him over, before they leave for lunch, to scold him, he knows he wasn't concentrating, but she's saying well done, she's holding out her hand, it's a pack of cards, a prize, for mastering his times tables, a few boys have stayed back, they're jostling around him, walking on either side of him, excitedly, begging him for a turn.

Across the fence, whistling cars, autumn sunlight.

| | | | | | |

It's 4 a.m. Cold air is blowing through the vents on the wall in the cell.

He's under the domed canopy, on his mother's lap, against the folds of yellow-brown bark. The thick aerial roots are protruding, like veins that grow from the trunk of the fig tree. The leaves, with their shiny oval faces, the underside burnished copper. He's leaning forward, to touch the roots that wrap themselves, down the sides of gullies and the edges of cliffs, rocks.

A torch is being shone, into each cell. For a minute, while he's still dreaming, his arms tucked against him on the sheet, he forgets.

| | | | | | |

In the mornings, he's blank, empty, when the guards walk from cell to cell, while he's still buried, mostly, inside the blanket. But on Saturday night, he wakes up, sweating despite the vents blowing almost-winter air, his dream is still fresh, more real than the fluorescent shadows, he's in the back seat of a car he doesn't recognise, he can hardly see out of the window, Evelyn is on the pavement, it's wet, Mitch is holding her hand, he's hitting his hand against the back window, Evelyn is crying, a woman he doesn't know is driving, she turns around, as if to stop, but the accelerator jolts and they move forward, he's hitting the window harder, harder, now the driver is screaming, he turns around, a final time, she's still there, with Mitch, but hazy, distant, sheeted by the sideways rain.

He doesn't know why, but after breakfast, he follows the others, to a small room, where they queue outside, a maximum of ten minutes each. There's a guard, with him, in the room, watching him, as he picks up the phone in his hand, gripping the coils, slowly dialling the mobile number she made him memorise, many times, just in case, now here he is, five rings, a brief pause and then a voice, so familiar, so distant, what his mum sounded like, or what he imagines she did, saying hello and then pausing, when she hears his voice, he's only got four minutes left, yes, next Saturday, it's only a few hours' drive, his cheeks are wet, the guard is pointing to his watch, walking over, to put the receiver back on the base, to escort him out, bring another one in.

| | | | | | |

All week, before she comes, he takes on extra tasks, clearing away, wiping the tables after dinner, as well as breakfast, mopping the floors after lunch. He volunteers to hand out the worksheets, his hand seems to go up faster than the other boys and after answering for the fourth time, he gets an elastic flicked at his back. He doesn't care, Ms Ali is going to give him a certificate, for his progress, talk to the admin office, he might even get extra credit, for the vending machine.

The night before Evelyn's visit, he barely talks to the others at dinner. He's in bed ten minutes after they're allowed to return to their cells, but at midnight, he's still listening to the boys shout through the glass, the guards ignoring them but then suddenly banging their knuckles against the locked doors, making notes in their logbook.

At 1 a.m., he's still awake, but his eyes are heavy, when he closes them, he can see horizontal lines inside his eyelids, then Mitch and him, playing, with putty, moulding it into shapes on the floor in Luke's bedroom. He's just turned five. They've only got one small container each, his mum's old shoe boxes, lining up their animals. Luke's are in the front, Mitch's animals in a neat row at the back of the cardboard box, Evelyn and his mum are in the kitchen, their voices rising and then evaporating, beneath the hiss of the rangehood.

Mitch has run out of putty, when Luke gets up to look out the window, Mitch reaches for the shoebox and grabs one of Luke's small animals, kneading it quietly between his fingers, to re-use for his own, Luke turns around, there's an empty space on the shoe box, the putty is still between Mitch's fingers, he's stepping back, the wooden rocking chair behind him, he's half-sitting, half-standing, over the chair, his arms stretched to the ceiling, dangling the putty, but too high for Luke to reach. Luke leans forward, edging closer to him, to the putty, but he accidentally steps on the shoebox, flying forwards onto Mitch, onto the chair, squashed putty shapes stuck to the heel of his shoes and then the chair goes over, backwards, and both boys land on the bedroom floor, half-crying, half-laughing, the chair lying silently beside them, its five wooden bars still intact, the cream pillow flopping forwards, as Evelyn and Mum rush from the kitchen to open the bedroom door.

In the morning, he's out of bed before the guards do their rounds, despite having barely slept, he makes his bed, folds his spare uniform, straightens the edge of the sheet that's come untucked, re-makes his bed, arranges the line of toiletries on his desk, this time in descending order, washes his hair, combs it, his mouth feels dry, he stands in front of the basin tap trying to wash a stain off his top, then realises it's an old stain, from before he wore it, spends another few minutes trying to dry his top, his head hurts, his throat is scratchy, he's still wiping the damp patch on his chest when the guard opens the door to his cell, to let him out for breakfast.

| | | | | | |

They'll check her ID, after the metal detector scans her bags, to check for explosives, firearms, pocket knives, scissors, ropes, lighters, flammable sprays, metal cutlery, no cameras, DVDs, CDs, laptops, USBs or other recording equipment. She'll have to hand her car keys to the guard, her handbag and phone go in the visitors' lockers. They'll make sure she has no gifts for him, no cigarettes, or drugs, alcohol or aerosols. No food from home either, though there is a vending machine if she wants to buy something to share. She'll have to take the packets and any leftover food with her, when she leaves. And if she shouts or uses offensive language, especially towards the guards, the visit is over.

She'll have to sit, in the same row of plastic chairs, waiting, until they are ready to bring her in, pausing, to the guard's annoyance, to buy two packets of crisps and two chocolates, from the vending machine at the end of the corridor.

He's in the room first, he can see her, approaching, through the glass.

| | | | | | |

When it's over, he watches her, his face pressed against the screen, as she makes her way back down the corridor, pausing to look back, a final time, before the guard opens the main door leading back to the admin office and then locks it, behind him, once Evelyn has passed through. He feels weightless, light-headed, as the guard leads him back, to join the others in the dining hall. She had fought for him, *every day since that woman took you*, she had promised his mum, she had tried, she's a single parent, she doesn't have money, or a big job, she's still renting, but she kept trying, she's still trying, she won't stop trying.

But after lunch, once they're back in their cells, before the afternoon programs, he starts to dip.

He can still see Evelyn's face, looking up to the ceiling, to blink, the red eye of the camera watching them, the sides of her fingers wiping small pools below her eyes, her cheekbones, her tears glassy beneath the fluorescent flicker: a magnetic ballast, pulsing, on and off, so quickly it seems the light is always on, but it's flickering, even if you can't see it. She is worried about him, but her face had looked drawn, sickly, still, like a fading photograph, as they sat beside each other, at the metal table, in an empty room, even the guard across the glass, tinged pale, green, by the bulbs, the long fluorescent tubes.

The adrenaline of the morning has worn off, his head feels worse, his throat is so sore he can barely swallow, he'd wanted to play with his cards, to calm him down, before dinner, but can't find the pack that he'd won, from Ms Ali, he'd hidden it under his bed, at first, under his uniform, then beneath the bible in the drawer of his desk, had he moved it again? Or had they come into his room, while he was meeting Evelyn? The sides of the bedframe, beneath his desk, his cupboard, bathroom, in the small gap behind the toilet, below the sink, under his pillow, his sheet, he's on his knees again, the skirting, the edges of the wall, they were jealous, they all wanted a turn, they were his, he can't get off the floor, he's pounding his feet against his desk, he can hear sounds from the passageway, approaching his cell, he rolls over, onto his side, pulling his legs towards his chest and then he remembers, that because it's Saturday, Clyde is on duty this evening.

| | | | | | |

The boy in the cell next to Luke doesn't speak, not often. Luke heard him one night, when a guard approached his cell, asking him questions with his logbook, but he talked so softly that the guard shook his head, closed the book and slammed his open palm against the glass. The guards call him The Baby, the others have taken up the name too, he wets his bed every night, the guards won't touch it, so he has to rinse the yellow patches himself under the tap before breakfast, and hang it over the back of his chair, the sheets are usually still damp, when they return to their cells at night.

Luke doesn't mind sitting next to him, tonight, he can smell the urine through his uniform, but at least he doesn't have to talk. They're facing each other, silent, while the guards change over, waiting for Clyde to say something or stand over them pointing his finger or take something off their plate, to eat it, laughing, in front of them. But tonight, he goes straight towards The Baby, his sheets are stinking out the whole passageway, he nearly passed out from the smell when he went to fetch the logbook, he's disgusting, he's dirtier than dog shit, he doesn't deserve to sleep in a bed. Clyde has wedged himself between the boy and Luke, he's sitting on the edge of the table, his leather boots are almost touching Luke's trainers.

The boy is crying now, nodding his head, he'll stop, he'll stop, but Clyde can't hear him, he bends down, closer, till his face is almost touching the boy's face, his arm hits Luke's elbow as he leans in further. The boy is crying more, more loudly, he can't help himself, he's wet his plastic chair, it's dripping down the thin metal legs of the chair, urine, pooling on the concrete floor, between his chair and Luke's. He looks down, Clyde's shoe is now encircled. The guard seems to sense something is wrong, he looks at boy, then at Luke, then down at his leather shoes, now sludgy, swimming, surrounded by a pool of urine.

Before he can take a breath, Clyde is off the table, pushing the trestle over onto its side, the boys hurrying out of their chairs, The Baby is lying face down, in his own urine, Clyde is kicking him, with his wet shoe, against his ribs, his back, his stomach. The other boys have formed a circle around them, some have turned their heads, but most are watching. Luke can't bear it, he's going to vomit, he gets down onto the ground, he's grabbing the boy's face out of the puddle, pulling him by the arms, dragging him across the concrete, away from Clyde's boots, the force of his legs, towards the turned over table nearby. Clyde pauses for a moment, as if in disbelief, before heaving himself towards the table, then lunging towards both boys, still lying on the ground, handcuffing Luke's right hand to the boy's left hand, forcing them up, grabbing the filthy dog, The Baby and his little sidekick, marching them in unison, past the door of the dining hall, down a long passageway, that connects to the Behavioural Management Section, or as he calls it for the boys, 'The Cage'.

| | | | | | |

He doesn't separate them until they're at
the end of the corridor, at the entrance to
the BMS, then Luke in one cell, the boy into
another, opposite him. There's more than one
cage, a row of cages, no glass panels to see in
or out of, just a few steel doors, connected by
a central passageway.
It's so dark when he enters the cell that he can't
see his own hands. Clyde shuts the door, leaving
him alone, motionless, standing, afraid to trip
over something or someone if he moves. After a
few minutes, there's a buzz, a loud hum
and a fluorescent tube, like the one in his usual cell,
clicks on, only this one, is fiercer, brighter,
impossible to make eye contact with, one
section of the tube seems about to short, it's
flickering incessantly, wheezing, blinding him
with its flashes, pulses. Maybe Clyde will turn it
off again, to punish him, to leave him in a small
dark box that he has to feel his way around,
with his hands, his legs, brushing against a bolted
chair, just a metal stool with no back, the frame
of a bed, bolted too, no mattress, no bedding,
no window, no bookshelf or bathroom, just an old
toilet, in the corner of the cell, with no seat, no
rim and no basin to wash his face. There are
names, crafted in small red squiggles, blood,
streaked on the wall beside the bed, they're
not allowed pens.

They told him, at breakfast, about a boy who hid
in his bathtub, for a whole year, after they released him,
he preferred it to his old bedroom, his mum
had to bring his meals, his pillow, to the bathroom.
The boys at the table next to him had sniggered,
overhearing them. He probably pissed in it, as well.
Clyde doesn't come back till morning. The fluorescent light
doesn't turn off. The Baby howls intermittently,
as if in pain, though his voice is muffled through
the steel frames. He is still lying, his legs curled
towards his chest, in the foetal position, on the metal frame
of the bed, when Clyde opens the door, just for a
moment, to put a stale roll and a plastic cup of water,
on a tray, on the floor, without even looking at him,
before he turns back and a few moment later,
The Baby's howling has stopped and Luke can hear the
door to his cell opening too. He needs to go, but
there's no toilet paper and when he looks up, he notices
a small video camera, that he hasn't seen before,
a one-eyed plastic frame, looking
down on him, from the high corner of the wall.

| | | | | | |

The day is fading into late afternoon,
he hasn't showered, or drunk, since the
bread roll this morning, The Baby has started
screaming again, though his cries
seem tired, softer.

His face feels numb, from his headache,
the flickering, the thirst, the pain in his ribs.

At lunchtime, he had banged on the steel
door, with his palms flat, then his knuckles
closed, then he'd slept, a few minutes at a
time, on the metal frame, beneath the
camera, waking up, thinking about The Baby
and Ms Ali, and Evelyn, who had promised to
come back in a fortnight, with Mitch too this time.

He comes past shortly before midnight,
throwing down a tray with another plastic
cup and a small bowl of mashed potato and
beans, laughing as the mash slides out of
the bowl, landing in small moulds and
streaks of hair, fluff, concrete.

| | | | | | |

Your bare feet, your teeth, your bones,
the intermittent shrieks from The Baby's
cell, the trays, the days passing, the
flickering, the spilt food, the smell,
the steel doors, slamming, the concrete,
the toilet that doesn't flush, the wall,
the names,
the camera, watching, always, the smell
of pepper spray, through the air vents,
the early mornings, the metal frame.

You have to dissociate, deaden,
withdraw like an ebbing tide.

| | | | | | |

Even his dreams seem stagnant,
he sees faces, his mum's, Evelyn's,
Mitch's, sometimes Mrs B, Emily,
Ms Ali, even Rae, holding
an umbrella or an old newspaper,
Magda, the chair in the study,
the maroon folds, her ashtray,
shaped like a dog, with a glue line,
holding it together, where it
smashed, it was all his fault really,
she said, it was accident, except
it wasn't, it's only an ashtray,
who cares? She did, even Nate
comes sometimes, to say I told
you so, to tell him to keep fighting,
cause he would have busted the
guard's balls by now, but then how
come he keeps going in and out
and in and out
of juvie, like a revolving toy.

| | | | | | |

The Baby is quiet today,
unusually so, Clyde seems
distracted and for once, he
doesn't spill the food, on
purpose, when he lowers the
tray to the floor.

| | | | | | |

It's going on ten days, he's keeping
a small row of leftover rice, from his
intermittent meals, his own abacus,
to mark the days, alone, a row
beneath the metal frame, they never
clean the cell, they never come, except
for Clyde, they won't notice, but he
might get ants and then, without
the abacus, he won't know, how long,
    how long.

| | | | | | |

He's scraping his thumb against
the paint, covering his eyes,
the sun is too bright, he's running
behind her, towards the fig trees
near the water, the small
fruit growing all year round,
transforming from yellow to
deep red, he's still in his school
uniform, he stops beneath the
tree, lying down, folding into a
ball under its broad canopy,
wrapping himself between the
folds of its aerial roots, running
his hands over the rusty velvet
underside, the leaves,
glossy limbs, she's calling
to come inside,
his pillow is damp,
it's still dark,
he can hear an alarm
through the glass,
like a school bell,
a train shrieking,

just a drill.

| | | | | | |

The mornings are ok,
but the nights   the early hours
lying flat, or on his side,
his knees to his chest
beneath the light that
dissolves and
then re-appears, without
pause, in the mornings,
he makes plans, he remembers,
forces himself, to think of them,
to imagine   Evelyn's next visit,
with Mitch, his next meal,
Ms Ali,
finding his cards,
the picture of his mum,
in the lockers still,
near the admin office,
to think about The Baby,
how he must be feeling
if he can stop himself,
wetting
the metal bed frame.

| | | | | | |

It's the late afternoons,
when he feels a blanket
of sadness, bathing
him, washing him,
gently
seeping into
him.

| | | | | | |

The Baby won't stop tonight,
    the doors keep banging
           there's no food on the evening tray
        just water
        burning light
        and the sound of steel,
          opening
                      closing

| | | | | | |

In his dream, they're together
she's holding
his hand,
adjusting the straps
of his school bag,
beside the yellow castle
and tower
but when he looks
up
it's
liquid
fire, flue
flames of
smoking rubbish

from the mouth,
the chute
they're covering,
coughing
trying to breathe
with their
hands
over their
faces,
she's shouting,
begging him to run,
towards the
school gates

she's on the ground,
the smoke has
surrounded her,
the sky is
filled
with burnt particles,
ash, clinker, steam

| | | | | | |

He can smash the light
in his cell
if
      he can reach it,
standing on the bolted

stool, then he can
think straight again

without the flicking,

flicking

of nights, days,
that presses
down   even
when his eyes are
shut

through his
eyelids,

his skull.

| | | | | | |

The light is too high
        he's an idiot
for even wishing
        or trying
to reach
the fluorescent
tube,
they're not
that dumb,

that's why,

the stool
is bolted, and
he saw
an ant, today
under
the metal frame,

finally,
like he thought
to steal
his row of rice,
one but
tomorrow,
more

| | | | | | |

When it
opens,
the
door   he
lunges

at the tray
at Clyde, screaming

like The Baby does
beneath

        the camera,
and the
  long tube,

the flickering,
clicking,
fluorescent
tongue

licking him in light

| | | | | | |

  Can The Baby
  hear him now?
It's his turn he's on
  the concrete
   the tray
  has turned over
    there's gravy
  and bread
  beside him
and, a upturned cup.
He can feel water
  at the edges of
  his mouth
Clyde is kicking him
   pulling
  at his arms
  Pulling him up
   from the floor

  then pushing
   him

  face down
   onto the
   stool,
   a stump,
   felled,
the small remains,
a metal tree trunk,
   bolted

            to concrete,
               in the
          middle of his cell,
       but below   rootless,
            decomposing

            His arms
                   are cuffed
             behind him
          the metal pressing,

          against his ribs,
        The guard is taking off
           his leather shoes.

Evelyn is peering through the rectangular glass, pushing against the handle, there are two police officers, on the bench outside the wooden doors of the Coroner's Court. The rows in the public gallery are almost empty, groups of them, four chairs each, bolted together, a sign on some, but most are free, waiting.

Outside, a long corridor, numbered court rooms, doors, dark suits crowding the waiting area, beneath a large clock and thin fluorescent tubes.

The carpet inside the courtroom is grey too, with thick vertical lines, a court officer stands beside the Coroner's chair, gesturing to the small crowd gathering inside. There are jugs of water, microphones, a phone with a knotted cord, a screen on the wall, plug points, a small dustbin lined with a plastic bag, multiple cameras, built into the corners of the court room.

She sits in the back row of the gallery, the wall behind her is peeling, dented. The lawyers' table towards the front of the court is long, made of the same wood as the doors. There's a large silver trolley, piled with manila folders, parked near the wall close by, above the trolley, a fluorescent bulb, flickering.

The room is almost silent, the air-conditioning unit rattles intermittently. Piles of papers are being spread out on the tables, shuffled, re-folded. There's a low partition to separate the witness box. The court officer is pouring a glass of water, for the Coroner.

The Coroner's Assistant is young; the Coroner is in his sixties. They rise as he enters, he's a Magistrate of the Local Court, they bow their heads in his direction. The lawyers sit in maroon swivel chairs, the Coroner's chair is also maroon, but thick, padded, stationary.

He's addressing the lawyers, they stand as he calls them. Evelyn is the only one in the back row, the police officers from outside have entered too, they're seated a few rows in front of her. The court officer is testing the microphones positioned on each table, then ushering in the first witness.

> L forcibly banged on the door of his cell with his shoes to attract C's attention. When C entered the cell, located in the Behavioural Management Section (BMS), L lunged towards him and attempted to assault him. C attempted to subdue and restrain L, on the bolted stool inside the cell (for L and C's protection). L fell backwards off the metal stool, onto the concrete floor, sustaining fatal injuries as a result.
>
> L was moved to the BMS following an earlier confrontation with C in the Centre's dining hall, and L's consequent threats of harm made against K, other guards and himself.

The entire gallery on the right hand side is unoccupied, rows and rows of chairs, empty. Other than the Coroner, his assistant, the lawyers, police, the waiting witnesses and the court officer, a handful of journalists are seated in the front row, a few observers behind them. It's an open court, but the chairs in front of her, like the other side of the gallery, are unoccupied.

> L's fragile mental state contributed to his forceful attempt at assaulting C. In addition, his overall poor physical health would have exacerbated the impact of the injuries sustained during his fall. It is not known if, in addition to his injuries, L had any other pre-existing health conditions that may have further contributed to his death.

There are no tape recorders, or cameras, allowed in. Evelyn's mobile phone is in her bag, switched off. They can enter, or leave, at any time, unless there's a sign on the door. But they mustn't move around or speak while the witnesses are taking the oath, or the affirmation. One of the journalists in front of her was at the front desk earlier, signing a form, to bring her laptop into court. The Coroner's assistant is calling the prison guard, C, to the witness box, he's swearing an oath, the journalist's fingers are pacing her laptop keys, then she's closing the screen, opening the wooden doors to answer her phone, returning a few minutes later, bowing as she re-enters.

He's been trained to work with young people, to help them get ready for real life, for adulthood, the workforce. He has tried to teach them the consequences of their offending, to help them live productive lives when they get back out in the community. Maybe on occasion he has overstepped the mark, taken a few practical jokes a bit far, but the boys know when he's joking, they respect him. He doesn't hold a grudge, they don't either. L was out of line, he dealt with him according to the rules of the Centre. He was separated as a punishment, for L's safety, the other boys', for his own safety. L's punishment was not excessive, he was not treated unfairly. L was a violent and unstable young offender, with complex mental health issues and ongoing behavioural problems. He did the best he could to work with that, to support L to understand appropriate boundaries and expectations. He took all the appropriate actions, before, during and after the tragic incident.

> Upon seeing that L had sustained serious injuries as a result of his fall, C immediately called the Centre nurse who attended the scene. First aid was urgently administered and CPR was performed on the deceased, as well as an ambulance being called. Unfortunately, despite their best efforts, L could not be revived. The attending nurse confirmed the death upon physical inspection of the body and confirmation that L was without a pulse.

The Director of the Centre enters the witness box next. He's led the institution for more than a decade. He has full confidence in his staff to manage difficult circumstances appropriately. C has been an outstanding guard, he doesn't believe in the over-use of force, but when you're dealing with these young offenders, sometimes you need to use some force. They can pose a risk, to themselves, to others, an unacceptably high risk, C would have taken that into consideration. The Director is tapping the soles of his shoes against the floor, softly, as he speaks. They are shiny, genuine leather, tightly grained, with low block heels and punch hole detailing. The circumstances that resulted in this, in L's death, we are addressing them ... we hope they won't be repeated.

> No CCTV footage of the inside of L's cell could be provided. At the time the request was made, the Centre advised that the footage in question had inadvertently been written over. This is unfortunate as it

would have been helpful to the investigation if such footage had been retained. Nonetheless, C's testimony was sufficiently comprehensive and has enabled a fuller understanding of the circumstances.

It's not possible to give an exact number, of how many are in segregated custody, on a given day. They keep a record, but it fluctuates, all the time, depending on what's happening, he doesn't want to misrepresent it, what today's figure is. The Director is shifting in his chair inside the witness box, his hands are tucked under his suit, his elbows on the plastic arm rests. The government has invested a substantial sum, over the past four years, to improve the system, they've expanded infrastructure in his Centre, and programs and services. But some of these young people are violent, complex, solitary confinement should always be a last resort, but responding to the needs of young people like L can be very challenging. L was a danger, to himself, to the guards, to the other young offenders, L was there for his own good. He's committed to working to create positive behaviour changes, but he's not going to apologise for wanting his Centre to be as safe as possible, for his staff and for the young people themselves.

> C's use of force was permitted given the immediate threat of harm posed by L. The risk of harm was so significant and imminent that there was, in all probability, no time for C to even consider alternative means of responding. That L fell backwards from the chair while being subdued (and consequently sustained life-threatening injuries) could not reasonably have been foreseen by C.

It's almost 4 p.m. Evelyn is sinking into her chair. The lid of her water bottle has fallen, she's reaching down, between the frames of the chairs to find it, there's something sticky, chewing gum or Blu-Tack, beneath the seats, on her fingertips, the lid is nowhere to be seen. The light above the guard has stopped flickering, it's gone out, Evelyn is blinking, to adjust her eyes. Her arms feel heavy, she's leaning back in her chair.

The Coroner's assistant is looking up too, she'll have to call maintenance after the hearing. They're almost done, the last witness has left the box, the findings have been read, it's late afternoon, the journalist is tapping her fingers on her laptop.

- I recommend that communications be sent to all staff at the Centre reminding them that solitary confinement for young offenders should only used as a last resort to ensure the safety and security of prisoners and staff;
- A clearer approval process to be developed to manage decisions regarding the length of time that young offenders may be held in solitary confinement and improve transparency;
- Department's policy (that any stays exceeding 24 hours in solitary confinement must be approved at an executive management level) be more rigorously enforced by the Centre;
- Staff to receive comprehensive training to increase their ability to manage challenging behaviours; improve communication and negotiation with youth offenders; and practice conflict management and managing unconscious bias, including techniques for de-escalation and incident management;
- Training to be provided to new staff as a mandatory module upon joining the Centre and existing staff should undertake a 'refresher' module annually;
- A new position be created within the Centre's Training Unit to conduct an annual systematic audit of all training offerings provided to ensure that staff are provided with the right training and to assess whether staff members' training records are up to date.

The lights that remain leave long shadows under the rows of chairs. The gallery is almost empty. There's a plastic cup on its side beside an empty seat, the carpet is damp. Her new shoes have given her blisters already, she's rubbing her right heel.

The Coroner is clearing his throat, addressing the court in a louder voice than before, the journalist in front sits upright, Evelyn is leaning forwards, facing the judge's bench.

> Although no witnesses were present during the altercation, there is no reason to suggest that C's actions were improper. Given L's actions and assumed state of mind, he posed an extremely high risk to C (and to himself). C consequently took steps to manage that risk by employing reasonable force, in accordance with the measures permitted by both the Centre and the Department's policies and procedures. I will not be recommending C for criminal prosecution or disciplinary action relating to this death in custody. However, the recommendations provided must be implemented by the Centre to prevent a future occurrence of this tragic nature. Our deepest sympathies are extended to the family and friends of L.

The Coroner rises, the Coroner's assistant stays behind, he exits through the door behind the maroon chair, Evelyn's chair snaps upright when she stands, the journalists are behind her, following her, someone is holding the wooden doors open so she can pass, the journalist with the laptop is standing in front of her, gesturing to the microphone, the light from a camera is shining in her eyes, her voice is raised, her cheeks are wet, the chairs in the waiting area have emptied, they're spilling onto the front steps of the court, the microphone is pressed against her lips, today is not the end, it's a mockery, she is never going to give up fighting for him, never, the guard deserves to be prosecuted, it's a tragedy but it's also a crime and she will keep on fighting for justice until, until.

The small crowd outside the Coroner's Court is dispersing, crossing the busy road, beside the university, not far from their old apartment building. A few journalists have stayed behind to talk to one another. Evelyn's throat is hoarse, her eyes are stinging, she's looking into the small mirror in her handbag, wiping away the smudges.

She doesn't have a hat with her; there is no shade from the late-afternoon sun.

She walks towards the overhead bridge, a little further on, students are crossing in small groups onto campus, the bells from the clocktower in the quadrangle are ringing, sandstone, gargoyles, bronze pipes, a graduation ceremony in the Great Hall. A group of first year students watching from outside. That will be Mitch, *next year*.

She's past the crowds, the streets have emptied, she's walking faster past bookshops and cafes, the streets have gentrified since they lived there, the rents have quadrupled. She's starting to cry again, the boys' old school is on left, she pauses, the memorial plaque is still there, the soldier, with the tilted hat, the rows of names.

Behind the fence, a group of primary children have stopped playing, they're watching her, gesturing through the bars of the school fence, she's wiping her cheeks, blowing her nose on her sleeve, mascara is streaked down her face, a teacher joins the children on the playground, calls them back inside.

Past the terraced streets, beneath rows of Port Jackson trees, their branches cast downwards, the pavements of fallen figs.

When she's calmer, she follows the path to the shoreline of Blackwattle Bay.

It's a different kind of harbour, greyer, more industrial, across the water from the fishmarket, new apartment buildings have replaced the warehouses and factories, above them, the thick steel threads of the Anzac Bridge. Iron, timber, abattoirs, the goods line bringing sugar and wheat to the boats, a distillery site, shipwrights, stone retaining walls, it's all there, just buried. To her left, his yellow castle, the tower, upright, imposing, like the entrance to a courthouse, she climbs the stone steps to get closer to the building.

She's holding onto the rail, sitting on the top step, the ground is cold, there are no benches, just a few shrubs nearby, the grass is getting long. It's hard to believe that beside her there was once fire and flue, ravenous furnaces, noxious fumes, no better than the rubbish barges or the quarries that came before, just a different kind of poison, neater, hidden, until the coughing, the complaints, the growing protests from residents, until the public tide turned against the old incinerator and it fell out of use.

They might have torn it down, despite its unusual modern façade, regenerated the land, but still the building stands, slightly shrunken, weathered, its true purpose almost forgotten, its frame intact.

It's a short flight to Canberra, she takes a taxi from the airport to their apartment. They moved there, soon after his death. Mitch was offered a sports scholarship for the rest of high school, she was happy to move away.

She's exhausted. Mitch is waiting for her at the front door, he puts his arm around her, he's got so tall, he towers over her. She closes the door behind them, there's a southerly coming, she goes over to close the window. In the corner is the rocking chair. She keeps a sheet over it, for the sun. It looks the same, other than a few missing chunks, it doesn't seem to have aged.

It needs a polish, the edges are splintering a bit, but it's in good condition. Mitch is in the kitchen making her a cup of tea. Her joints have stiffened, the chair is quite low, it takes her a few minutes to sit down, without hurting her back. Mitch is passing her the saucer, she needs the bathroom, but she can't get up. She drinks the tea anyway, she's too tired to talk.

It's not your fault Mum, you did everything you could.

She's reaching over to the small table beside her, she's lighting a candle. She's barely rocking, her head is bent forwards, her hands are pressed against her forehead, her tears are falling onto her lap.

He takes her empty cup to the sink, the room is getting colder, he's got to go upstairs to study, he's got exams in a week. She's still there, in the chair, he can't leave her.

He sits in the chair beside her, his hands in her hands. They're almost twice the size of hers. They're linking their fingers together, like they used to do, her tears are dripping onto his hands now. He wipes them away gently.

The room is dark, except for the small glow from the flame, wax is dripping onto the edges of the table, neither of them gets up to wipe it or turn on the light. After a while, he can hear her snoring, the candle has burnt out, he loosens his hands slowly, to find the light on his phone, he fetches a blanket from the couch to cover her, small burnt flakes have fallen from the wick onto the floorboards beside the couch.

She's still asleep in the chair when Mitch comes down for breakfast in the morning.

| | | | | | |

      the guard's shoe hits his spine first,

                      an ankle-high boot
leather, skin,

dyed, hardened, swung and rapped   against bone,
in a jagged vertical line

                    from his coccyx,   his sides,
up to his neck

there's nylon too, in the upper part,

            side zipper, adjustable, waterproof

    and a lug sole, polymer, thick rubber,

                        with deep indentations for grip,

| | | | | | |

        the pain moves   in circles

    when it seems to be over,
Clyde comes back   towards him,   again
with his muscular legs
                    and the leather boot

    When he catches a breath,

he looks up,   but it's   a mistake
the light is against him
    too,

it's escaped   the rectangular tube,
 that had fixed it to the ceiling,

its spiralling   across the cell,

like an open fist, a glowing palm, punching the air, cheering Clyde on,

              the guard's cheeks reflecting,
                  the luminous, crimson
            heat,

              as he throws him
                  off the bolted stool,
            the metal stump

his hands still cuffed behind him,
                  face-down

        onto
                the concrete,

> he always thought
> > That the fig trees only bloomed
> > > > once a year
>
> but his mum said twice,
> > > summer and autumn,
> > two crops
>
> > the tree,
> has never been barren or cursed,
>
> in drought, excessive heat,
> > > the fig wasp,
>
> > birds, flying foxes
> peck the tiny-flowered fruit,
>
> > > > like blood, the scarlet skin

| | | | | | |

               there's a boot   against his neck,

                  He can't draw   breathe,

         He can taste the same blood   in his mouth,

that snakes in small streams, expanding puddles   that meander
                                                   across the concrete   floor

       he can feel the guard standing
       over

him,
him,

watching,

         then reaching upwards   perched on the metal frame,
      to the tiny eye,
                  the video camera, the corner of the wall, high

then glass, falling, splinters,

like flakes of hard skin   from the ceiling edges,

the steel door to his cell,

                 closing, echoing
                        in its frame,

| | | | | | |

        full, or partial shade,
              blunt-tipped, smooth,

      mites and scales,

   and soil that isn't properly drained
                           can seize the roots   and rot
  still, they grow, into the ground, thickening,

        near forests, estuaries, rocky outcrops

                      along the coast

buttressed, supporting the branches

free of thorns, sometimes pruned, for power lines
in sandy or acidic ground,

                          evergreen, standing.

| | | | | | |

His mum is in the room with him, she's going   to call his teacher,
          after she's wiped the blood that's raining from his nostrils,

They'll take   a walk, together,   to cheer him up,

              to turn on the
              steps outside,

hand in hand,   go anywhere they like,
she   just needs to slip on her   comfy shoes,   the walking pair,
                                       he's already got his on,

they can invite Evelyn and Mitch, too, if they're free,

she's leaning back, the chair is rocking,   slightly,
                                   as she laces her trainers,
the mid-morning light is gentle, they don't need their hats,   just yet,

the street is soft, purple,   blue still damp,   from the midnight
                                                           downpour,
                              that had   woken him up,
and drowned the fallen jacaranda leaves,

and sent him,   down the corridor to open her door,
and beg her
not to leave him alone,   with his lamp off,

after   a while,   sandstone, brick, corrugated iron, woven into
elaborate shapes, hanging lamps, re-painted facades,
she steps ahead to look,   he loses sight   of the back of her hat,
it's somebody else's,
then,   his shoes,   his   shoes,
into the watery-purple trumpets—
dissolving—
unyielding—
but dissolving—
broken, spongy—
the residue—of wet leaves—
beneath his shoes—his shoes,
—his   s-kin.

Afterword

The Leaves brings together many years spent studying, researching and working in my two areas of specialisation – literature and law. My PhD in literature explored the representation of historical trauma (particularly in relation to the Holocaust) through the form of the novel. I also considered the intersections between ethics and interpretation in literary, legal and historical narratives.

The part time job that I held at a legal organisation while studying prompted my initial awareness of youth detention issues and the frequent interrelation between the foster system, homelessness and imprisonment. Made up of specialists, magistrates and defence lawyers for incarcerated children, the legal committee that I supported for several years was dedicated to promoting the rights of incarcerated children and making submissions in relation to youth justice policy. The business of the committee gave me a different, real-world perspective on the jurisprudential issues that I would learn about in the classroom as a law student. It also instilled in me a deep sense of how important it is to reform young offenders in a way that is genuinely restorative and effective and that acknowledges the traumatic legacy of colonialism underpinning our history.

The Leaves highlights the brutal, outdated and punitive 'Victorian-era' approach to youth justice that persists to this day.

While I have done a significant amount of research, *The Leaves* is not based on any one particular incident or case. Rather, the protagonist is a kind of 'Everyman'—the personification of hundreds and hundreds of deaths 'inside' that have occurred since the 1991 Royal Commission and for which there has been no justice or accountability.

This is partly why I decided to call the novel *The Leaves*, when the Jacaranda tree is usually synonymous with the vibrant purple blooms that appear in early summer for a fleeting season. I wanted to make the often-unnoticed Jacaranda leaves 'visible', to highlight the voiceless youth incarcerated in our brutal detention system. I hope the title might shift the reader's focus from the blooms to the leaves, to consider what has been lost (in Luke's case—his mother, his childhood and innocence, his freedom and ultimately his life) and to confront what is genuinely broken in our legal and social structures.

This work, which involves contending with the lingering impact of colonialism on our contemporary justice system, still lies ahead. At present, more than three decades since the Royal Commission, very few of the recommendations to prevent further Indigenous deaths in custody have actually been implemented. The statistics continue to be distressing and are likely to remain so unless, as a nation, we can find a way to genuinely engage with and address this urgent issue of our times. For me, the novel is an innately political form that can participate in this kind of critical cultural discourse. Kafka spoke of literature as the 'axe' that can thaw 'the frozen sea inside us'. It is my hope that *The Leaves* might play a small role in this conversation, advocating for a more empathetic and humane approach to how our society reforms young offenders.

Other books available from Spinifex Press

Trauma Trails, Recreating Song Lines:
The Transgenerational Effects of Trauma in Indigenous Australia

Judy Atkinson

Shortlisted, 2003 Australian Awards for Excellence in Educational Publishing

I was running a workshop in the Kimberleys, and in the circle a woman began to speak from a place of deep pain and despair. She described herself as bad, dirty, ugly, words she had taken into herself from childhood experiences of abuse. I lent forward and sang her a song. "How could anyone ever tell you, you are anything less than beautiful ..." While sitting with her, as the words settled into her soul, another woman said to the circle: you are recreating song lines—from trauma trails. I was honoured by this description of my work.

Providing a startling answer to the questions of how to solve the problems of generational trauma, *Trauma Trails* moves beyond the rhetoric of victimhood, and provides inspiration for anyone concerned about Indigenous and non-Indigenous communities today. Beginning with issues of colonial dispossession, Judy Atkinson also sensitively deals with trauma caused by abuse, alcoholism and drug dependency.

Then, through the use of a culturally appropriate research approach called Dadirri (listening to one another), Judy presents and analyses 'stories of pain, stories of healing', and is able to point both Indigenous and non-Indigenous readers in the direction of change.

"What *Trauma Trails* ultimately offers is a pathway to healing through the listening to, and telling of, stories that is based in Indigenous cultural and spiritual practices (the We-Ali program). This book speaks to the wisdom of the elders, to the incredible strength of Indigenous peoples, and to the enduring power of women."
—Ambelin Kwaymullina, Australian Women Writers

ISBN 9781876756222

Kick the Tin

Doris Kartinyeri

I understand why there is a lot of hatred in the Aboriginal community where children have been forcibly removed from their families by white governments. How could anyone think that apologies or money could make up for the lost years and the terrible trauma and emotional damage caused to my family?

When Doris Kartinyeri was a month old, her mother died. The family gathered to mourn their loss and welcome the new baby home. But Doris never arrived to live with her family—she was stolen from the hospital and placed in Colebrook Home, where she stayed for the next fourteen years.

The legacy of being a member of the Stolen Generations continued for Doris as she was placed in white homes as a virtual slave, struggled through relationships and suffered with anxiety and mental illness.

'Kick the Tin' was a game Doris played in the Colebrook Home. Hers is a life that has been kicked around. And it is the compelling story of a courageous journey of one woman into her soul to find meaning after the loss of everything the rest of us take for granted.

"[Kick the Tin] is a story of courage and survival, powerfully demonstrating how the human spirit can soar despite all the injuries and injustices which threaten to drag it down."
—Lowitja O'Donoghue

ISBN 9781875559954

Karu: Growing Up Gurindji

Violet Wadrill, Biddy Wavehill Yamawurr, Topsy Dodd Ngarnjal and Felicity Meakins

Gurindji country is located in the southern Victoria River in the Northern Territory of Australia. Gurindji people became well known in the 1960s and 1970s due to their influence on Australian politics and the Indigenous land rights movement. They were instrumental in gaining equal wages for Aboriginal cattle station employees and they were also the first Aboriginal group to recover control of their traditional lands.

In *Karu*, Gurindji women describe their child-rearing practices. Some have a spiritual basis, while others are highly practical in nature, such as the use of bush medicines. Many Gurindji ways of raising children contrast with non-Indigenous practices because they are deeply embedded in an understanding of country and family connections. This book celebrates children growing up Gurindji and honours those Gurindji mothers, grandmothers, assistant teachers and health workers who dedicate their lives to making that possible.

"*Karu: Growing Up Gurindji* shares the cultural knowledge, language and experiences of some extraordinary women and their roles as matriarchs, aunties, sisters and health workers. Karu gives new meaning to the phrase 'bedtime stories' with Dreamtime stories about Gurindji country, its creatures, and the morals followed to live a rich life. This book, accompanied by striking photos and artwork, is not only a gift to mothers, but everyone who values children."
—Dr Anita Heiss, Wiradjuri Nation, author and Professor of Communications, University of Queensland

"Beautifully written by First Nations women on Gurindji country where the fight for equal wages began. This book passionately expresses the stories told by strong women about their history and culture. A must read!"
—Senator Malarndirri McCarthy, Yanyuwa Nation, Senator for the Northern Territory

ISBN 9781925581836

*If you would like to know more about
Spinifex Press, write to us for a free catalogue, visit our
website or email us for further information
on how to subscribe to our monthly newsletter.*

Spinifex Press
PO Box 105
Mission Beach QLD 4852
Australia
www.spinifexpress.com.au
women@spinifexpress.com.au